P9-CDA-798

Letters
from
Camp

Other Books by
Kate Klise
illustrated by
M. Sarah Klise

REGARDING THE FOUNTAIN

Letters from Camp

By **KATE KLISE**

ILLUSTRATED BY M. SARAH KLISE

HarperTrophy®
A Division of HarperCollinsPublishers

HarperTrophy® is a registered trademark of HarperCollins Publishers Inc.

Letters from Camp
Text copyright © 1999 by Kate Klise
Interior illustrations copyright © 1999 by M. Sarah Klise
Layout and design by M. Sarah Klise with assistance from Matthew Willis

All rights reserved. No part of this book may be reproduced in any
manner whatsoever without written permission except in the case of
brief quotations embodied in critical articles or reviews.
Printed in the United States of America.
For information address HarperCollins Children's Books, a division of
HarperCollins Publishers, 10 East 53rd Street, New York, NY 10022

Library of Congress Cataloging-in-Publication Data
Klise, Kate.
    Letters from camp / Kate Klise; illustrated by M. Sarah Klise.
      p.   cm.
    Summary: Sent to Camp Happy Harmony to learn how to get along with each other,
pairs of brothers and sisters chronicle in letters home how they come to suspect the
intentions of the singing family running the camp.
    ISBN 0-380-97539-4.—ISBN 0-380-79348-2 (pbk.)
    [1. Camps—Fiction. 2. Brothers and sisters—Fiction. 3. Letters—Fiction. 4. Mystery
and detective stories.]
I. Klise, M. Sarah, ill.   II. Title.
[PZ7.K684Le   1999]
[Fic]—dc21   98-52315
                                                                                 CIP
                                                                                 AC

First HarperTrophy edition, 2000
❖
Visit us on the World Wide Web!
www.harperchildrens.com
11 12 13 OPM 20 19 18 17 16 15

This book is dedicated to our sisters,
Elizabeth, Molly, Julia,
and our brother, James,
without whom
life would be unimaginable.

"3 or 4 Families in a Country Village is the very thing to work on."

-Jane Austen

Letters from Camp

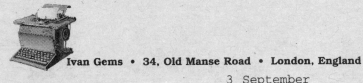

Ivan Gems • 34, Old Manse Road • London, England

3 September

Ms. Paige Turner
Publisher, #1 Books R Us
Avenue of the Americas
New York, New York USA

Dear Ms. Turner,

   Here is my manuscript. I'm calling it
Letters From Camp.

   I didn't make any changes to the notes or
letters. I just put everything in chrono-
logical order, as you suggested. I think
you'll agree that the letters speak for
themselves.

   I always thought I wanted to write novels, but you were right when you said the
truth sometimes makes a better story.
Besides, I couldn't make up half the things
that happened at camp — the secrets, the
songs, the sinister stroganoff.... But I'm
getting ahead of myself and the mystery.

   Enjoy the enclosed manuscript. I look
forward to hearing from you soon.

                    With kind regards,

                    Ivan Gems
                    Ivan Gems

P.S. I'd like to dedicate this book to the
friends I made at camp, all of whom became
like brothers and sisters to me, and to my
sister Mimi, who became a friend.

P.P.S. If any of my writing makes me sound
like an amateur, would you be so kind to
edit it? As you know, this is my first
mystery. I really hadn't planned on publishing until I was at least 14.

This is the ad that started it all. ←

ADVERTISEMENT

Are Your Children Suffering from an Inharmonious Relationship?

Take this short quiz to find out.

	YES	NO
Do your children fight a lot?	❑	❑
Do they call each other unattractive or even obscene names?	❑	❑
Is car travel difficult because of backseat wars between siblings?	❑	❑
Do you worry your children will never form the life-long sibling bond that joins two hearts together?	❑	❑

If you answered "YES" to one or more of the above questions, your children may be suffering from an inharmonious sibling relationship.

Don't worry. The Harmony Family Singers can help.

For more information about treating inharmonious sibling relationships, please write to us at:

**Camp Happy Harmony
601 Melody Lane
Harmony Hills, Missouri**

PAID FOR BY CAMP HAPPY HARMONY
A BRAND-NEW SUMMER CAMP WITH AGE-OLD VALUES

CHUCK ROAST RANCH

No Meal Is Complete Without A Little Red Meat

June 5

The Harmony Family Singers
Camp Happy Harmony
601 Melody Lane
Harmony Hills, Missouri

Howdy!

Just saw your ad in the back of *Ranching Round Up.* I'm sending my twins to your camp — pronto!

Their names are Barbie Q. and Brisket. Good kids, I reckon. I just worry neither one of them will amount to a hill of pinto beans.

The boy's as lazy as a slug. He sits in front of that dadburn TV, eating junk food like a cow chewing its cud. And Barbie Q.'s just the opposite. She's as spirited as a wild mustang, but her language could make a palomino blush. Her poor sweet mother would roll over in her grave if she saw the ratty clothes Barbie Q.'s been wearing lately. The girl says she's allergic to dresses.

And if that don't burn your bacon, Brisket and Barbie Q. fight like starving dogs over a T-bone.

They're yours for a month. Send me the bill, and I'll send you the wampum.

Good luck, pardners!

Chow,

Chuck "Wagon" Roast

Chuck "Wagon" Roast
Porterhouse, Texas

Try some gravy on your cold cereal!

Jewely Gems   34, Old Manse Road   London, England

15 June

Camp Happy Harmony
601 Melody Lane
Harmony Hills, Missouri USA

Sir or Madam:

I recently read about your camp in the pages of *Aristocracy Now*.

For your information, my daughter Mimi refuses to go to bed before midnight. She idles in her room for hours, drawing and painting childish scenes. My son Ivan is equally lacking in social skills. Last summer he stayed in his wing of the house for weeks on end, reading countless mystery novels.

I trust your staff will be able to correct these deficiencies. And I do hope you can find some way to discourage the children from bickering. It's so unattractive.

Do with the children as you will. I shall be in France for the summer.

Exclusively yours,

I am,

Jewely Gems

Jewely Gems

15 June

...appy Harmony $ $4,500.00

Four thousand five hundred and no/100 dollars (U.S.)   *Dollars*

Bank Of Old Money
London, England

For Summer Camp for I. and Mi.   *Jewely Gems*

4

June 18

Camp Happy Harmony
601 Melody Lane
Harmony Hills, Mo.

Dear Camp Director,

     After much reflection, we have decided to send our only children, Charlotte and Charlie, to your summer camp.

     They are delightful kids. We hope you won't think we're bragging when we tell you they both do very well in school. We're also pleased that Charlotte and Charlie are well-liked by their teachers and classmates. The only people they don't get along with are each other.

     We've tried everything we can think of to help our children be friends. Much to our sadness, nothing has worked.

     We'll miss them, but we think your camp is the last chance our children have to mend their troubled relationship. It is our deepest hope that Charlotte and Charlie will learn to feel for each other the love and care we feel for them.

     Yours sincerely,

Peter and Jane Lee

P.S. We know you've probably heard this a million times, but when we were kids, we never missed your TV show. We still play your old records. (That is, when the children aren't here.) As we said above, Charlotte and Charlie are great kids, but the music they listen to is . . . well, *very* modern. In fact, their taste in music is the only thing they share.

5

Rural Route 1, Box 257
Stopsign, Illinois

Send acceptance
letter to:
- Peter + Jane Lee
- Jewely Gems
- Chuck Roast

...nd ...

...y Singers are pleased to inform
...d for enrollment in a four-week
...g new Camp Happy Harmony.

...unhappy brothers and sisters redis-
...p. We love it when we can turn a pair
of squab... ...balanced duo of melody and harmony!

We're also delight... ...ur campers a taste of rural life. For one month, your children will milk go... s, gather eggs, and experience the joys of country living on an honest-to-goodness working farm. That's why we call our program *"The Camp That Works!"*

During their final week with us, your children will take part in a survival camping experience (Wilderness Adventure Week), when they'll reflect on the sibling skills they've learned during their stay.

You're invited back on the last day of camp (July 29th) for Sibling Appreciation Day. Just wait till you hear your children tell you in their own words the valuable lessons they've learned here at Camp Happy Harmony. You'll tingle with pride as you watch your kids perform the Harmony family theme song, *"We'd Rather Sing Than Fight, 'Cause Being Polite Is Such A Delight."* (Videotapes of the performance will be available for $29.95.)

Enclosed please find travel arrangements for your children, as well as a brochure about Camp Happy Harmony. We look forward to meeting your youngsters and sharing with them the Harmony secrets of sibling happiness!

Here's to a harmonious summer!

Sincerely,

Dorothy Harmony

Dorothy Harmony
Director of Admissions and "America's Favorite Soloist"

Come Away to
CAMP HAPPY HARMONY

Where the Hills Are Alive with the Sound of Happy Siblings

For almost four decades, The Harmony Family Singers have been singing their way into the hearts and homes of families everywhere.

Their weekly television show, "Harmony Begins At Home," was a must-see for an entire generation of children who grew up adoring the six multi-talented Harmony kids.

But the Harmonys were about more than just music. Their loving relationship with one another was an inspiration to families around the world.

Parents encouraged their children to model their relationships after the Harmony family's "close harmony." The family theme song, *"We'd Rather Sing Than Fight, 'Cause Being Polite Is Such A Delight,"* was a No. 1 hit on the pop charts for 64 weeks. The song became the motto for a nation in love with the sweet sounds of Harmony.

After their television show was canceled, The Harmony Family Singers pursued other careers. But whether selling water purification systems, pest control devices or home cleaning products, the Harmonys never abandoned their melodious mission: "To make *your* family as happy as *our* family."

Just last year the Harmonys returned home to the heartland of America, where their mission continues even today. Surrounded by the majestic beauty of the Ozark Mountains, the Harmonys established a summer camp for siblings who find themselves in inharmonious relationships.

"When we were children, we came into the homes of millions of fans," explains Dorothy Harmony, lead vocalist for The Harmony Family Singers. "Now we're inviting children to come to our home in the hills so we can share with them the secrets of family harmony."

"Look how we've changed! But we're still best friends!"

The Harmonys — 25 years ago

The Harmonys — Today

"We'd Rather Sing Than Fight, 'Cause Being Polite Is Such a Delight"
Still Singing the Same No. 1 Song that Made them Famous!

And now the Harmonys have opened a summer camp for kids!

CAMP HAPPY HARMONY

Staff

Camp Happy Harmony is a family-owned and operated camp. Our staff consists of members of the Harmony family. The only exception is **Lyle Splink**, our former sound engineer and bus driver. Now Lyle delivers camp mail to both sides of Lake Harmony — by canoe!

Activities

Swimming, boating, archery, crafts, singalongs.... You name it, we've got it! Everything, that is, except video games and cable TV. Don't worry. You won't even miss them once you get to Camp Happy Harmony.

Wardrobe Abode

Don't worry about packing. Our youngest sister and resident fashion plate, **Darlene**, will provide all the clothes you'll need during your stay. Darlene has taken many of our old stageclothes from our TV days and created a kooky, kicky line of Kamp Klothes. Kids love 'em!

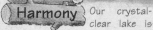

Cabins

You'll find our brothers' bunks ❷ on the east side of Lake Harmony. This is where the Harmony brothers (Dwayne, Dale and Daryl) teach boys the rights and responsibilities of a good brother. Our sisters' chalets are on the west side of the lake. That's where you'll find those songbirds of Harmony (Dorothy, Dolly and Darlene) sharing their secrets on how to be happy, helpful sisters. ❸

Lake Harmony

Our crystal-clear lake is ideal for swimming, boating and fishing. Twins **Dale and Daryl** (they're the athletes of the family) teach kids how to swim like a fish and fish like a pro in beautiful Lake Harmony! ❹

"America's Favorite Soloist"

"Try my cornbread!"

"I'm the stylish sister!"

Melody Mansion

You can't miss the Mansion. ❺ This neo-antebellum beauty is the prettiest building on the 200-acre Harmony estate. Our 350-seat theater occupies the first floor of the Mansion. Administrative offices are on the second floor. That's where **Dorothy** (yep, she's still the brains of the Harmony family) runs the show. The Melody Mansion is also home to the Harmony Family Hall of Fame, where we keep a complete collection of all our chart-busting records, videotapes and compact discs. We encourage campers to come to the Mansion in their free time to watch tapes of our old TV show and listen to the sweet sounds of Harmony. (♪Please note: No other music or television programming is permitted on the grounds of Camp Happy Harmony. Telephones are available to camp personnel only.)

Mail

Parents, don't be surprised when you receive letters from your children. We have a rule that campers must write at least one (1) letter home per week. Outgoing letters may be deposited in any of our camp mail boxes. We'll take care of the rest. Happy Harmony Camp-O-Gram stationery is provided free of charge for inter-camp mail. Besides teaching good manners, writing letters is a darn good habit for children to practice. As we all know, the key to any good relationship is COMMUNICATION!

Nature Trails

Daryl leads educational nature tours of our 200-acre property. You'll love learning about the flora and fauna of the Ozarks, especially when you can explore the wilderness while riding one of our burros!

Meals

If you thought **Dolly** could sing, just wait till you taste her cooking! We're proud to have a master chef in the family. Dolly prepares all meals at Camp Happy Harmony using only the freshest ingredients, many homegrown in our very own organic vegetable garden and orchard. ❻ All recipes used at Camp Happy Harmony were developed by **Dwayne**, our nutritional counselor. (This brother has a degree in good cookin'!) Three square meals (no between-meal snacks) are served daily in our very own **Wisteria Cafeteria**. ❼

DWAYNE

"I'm a health nut. Are you?"

DALE   DARYL

"We're those loveable twins!"

Mummy,

It happened again. Mimi tore the last page from the mystery on my night stand. Will you please DO something about her? Really, I can't live like this.

Ivan

Big Daddy-
Barbie Q. kicked me again today with them dang steel-toed boots.
Call the LAW!
Brisket

CHARLOTTE'S ROOM
MUTANTS, RODENTS AND OTHER GROSS CREATURES ARE NOT ALLOWED IN MY ROOM. (CHARLIE, THIS MEANS YOU!)

LIKE I'D WANT TO COME IN ANYWAY.

LISTEN, BIG DADDY!
Brisket called me a horse's patoot again today.

Spittin' mad,
Barbie Q.

Dearest Ivan,
If you put marmalade in my watercolours again, you shall not live to regret it.
Mimi

IVAN GEMS

10

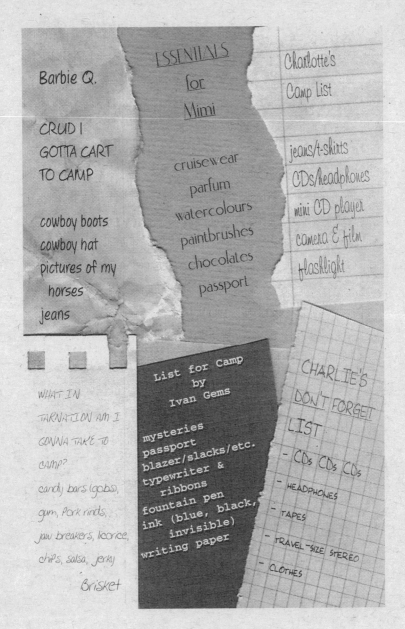

Barbie Q.

CRUD I
GOTTA CART
TO CAMP

cowboy boots
cowboy hat
pictures of my
  horses
jeans

ESSENTIALS
for
Mimi

cruisewear
parfum
watercolours
paintbrushes
chocolates
passport

Charlotte's
Camp List

jeans/t-shirts
CDs/headphones
mini CD player
camera & film
flashlight

WHAT IN
TARNATION AM I
GONNA TAKE TO
CAMP?
candy bars (gobs),
gum, pork rinds,
jaw breakers, licorice,
chips, salsa, jerky
  Brisket

List for Camp
by
Ivan Gems

mysteries
passport
blazer/slacks/etc.
typewriter &
  ribbons
fountain pen
ink (blue, black,
  invisible)
writing paper

CHARLIE'S
DON'T FORGET
LIST

- CDs CDs CDs

- HEADPHONES

- TAPES

- TRAVEL-SIZE STEREO

- CLOTHES

TEXAS TRAINS-PORTATION
"We Git You There LICKETY-SPLIT!"

TEXAS TRAINS-PORTATION
"We Git You There LICKETY-SPLIT!"

july 1   ONE WAY

FROM: PORTERHOUSE, TX
TO: HARMONY HILLS, MO   B/ROAST

HOMETOWN BUS SERVICE
SERVING SMALL TOWN AMERICA FOR AS LONG AS WE CAN REMEMBER

PASSENGER NAMES: CHARLOTTE & CHARLIE LEE*
DATE OF TRAVEL: JULY 1

LEAVE/STOPSIGN, IL.....................................8:07 A.M.
ARRIVE/HARMONY HILLS, MO......................7:17 P.M.

PRICE: $48.00

*PASSENGERS HAVE REQUESTED SEATS ON OPPOSITE SIDES OF BUS

WITH STOPS IN PEORIA, PEKIN, PADUCAH, PALMYRA, POTOSI, PURDY & HARMONY HILLS

NAME OF PASSENGER
GEMS/IVAN
FROM
LONDON/HE
TO
HAR

ISSUED BY **ENGLISH AIR INTERNATIONAL**
PASSENGER TICKET AND BAGGAGE CHECK   CHECK-IN REQUIRED

NAME OF PASSENGER
GEMS/MIMI
FROM
LONDON/HEATHROW
TO
HARMONY HILLS REGIONAL AIRPORT

english Air international

DATE
JULY 1
CLASS
FIRST
FLIGHT #
1807

Week 1

Notes for Orientation:

Week of July 2 - 8

THINGS TO DO THIS WEEK:

I. Welcome (My solo: "Look At Me, I'm Dor-o-thy!") Open with "We're Glad you're here" yadayodayoda

II. Introduce Harmony family (My solo: "Meet My Family!")

III. Hello, campers (My solo: "Now Let's Get To Know You!") Have kids introduce themselves. Note any buds in need of early nipping.

IV. Discussion of camp rules (My solo: "It's Understood: You'll Be Good -- Or Else")

V. Close (All Harmony number: "We'd Rather Sing than Fight, 'Cause Being Polite Is Such A Delight")

14

CAMP HAPPY HARMONY LEDGER

Week of July 2 - 8

DATE	DESCRIPTION	✓	+ INCOME	− EXPENSES
7/2	Tuition		13,500.00	
7/3	Royalties		54.89	
			13,554.89	
7/3	Director's salary			2,000.00
7/4	Other staff salary			1,000.00
7/5	Advertising/marketing			7,500.00
7/6	Groceries (for us)			365.49
7/6	Groceries (for kids)			25.29
7/7	Miscellaneous expenses			200.00
				11,090.78

Balance : $2,464.11

Gourmet Goodies
Fabulous Food for Fabulous People

foie gras
escargot (30 lbs.)
paté with bacon and walnuts
cantaloupe sherbet
raspberries
croissants
linguine + fresh lobster sauce
prime rib
marmalade
chocolate cheesecake

TOTAL: $365.49
DELIVER TO CAMP HAPPY HARMO
(back entrance) — C/O DOROTHY

BEAUTY HUT
The Ozarks' House of Beauty

Client Name: Dorothy Harmony
Dorothy Harmony
anti-wrinkle facial
eyebrow waxing
Fee: $125.

Just Be-Claws
Nails For People Who Need 'Em!

mer: Dorothy Harmony
ure + pedicure: $75.

SAVE-MORE WHOLESALE FOODS
Damaged and Dented
But Still Pretty OK Groceries

cereal . . . . 2@2.09
bread (week old) . . . . 3@.99
peanut butter 2.99
jelly 2.10
macaroni . . . . 5@.89
beans . . . . 2@1.69
rice . . . . 3@1.74

COST : $25.29

WEEK ONE
CLASS SCHEDULE

SISTERS	BROTHERS

Monday

Fishing for Compliments	Dressing to Impress Sis
Instructor: Darlene	Instructor: Dale
Place: Lake Harmony	Place: Wardrobe Abode

Tuesday

Bedtime Tantrums	Mind Your Manners!
Instructor: Dolly	Instructor: Dwayne
Place: Wisteria Cafeteria	Place: Melody Mansion
Letters home due today	

Wednesday

Clothes Make the Sister	Daryl Does the Outdoors
Instructor: Darlene	Instructor: Daryl
Place: Wardrobe Abode	Place: Nature Trails

Thursday

Sing-Along with the Harmony Gals	I'm Terrific, So Are You!
Instructor: Dorothy	Instructor: Daryl
Place: Melody Mansion	Place: Wisteria Cafeteria

Friday

Phoo on Fussy Eating!	Singing for Health
Instructor: Dolly	Instructor: Dwayne
Place: Wisteria Cafeteria	Place: Melody Mansion

Saturday

Pardon Me, but the Dinner Table is NOT a Horse Stable	Let's Swim!
Instructor: Dolly	Instructor: Dale
Place: Wisteria Cafeteria	Place: Lake Harmony
	Letters home due today

Sunday

Rest and Relaxation	Rest and Relaxation
All-Camp Evening Sing-Along	All-Camp Evening Sing-Along

ACTIVITIES
WEEK ONE

GIRLS	BOYS
wash dishes (all meals)	gather eggs
clean barns/ chicken coop (daily)	feed pigs/ groom burros
milk goats (twice per day)	clear rocks from riding trails
scrub & wax all floors	clean septic lines
weed vegetable garden	vacuum (all buildings)
renovate cafeteria	re-roof barn
remove algae from lake	bale hay in pasture
write one letter home	write one letter home

WEATHER FORECAST:

Sunny and hot. Highs in the mid-80s. Lows in the mid-60s. No rain expected this week.

THIS WEEK AT THE WISTERIA CAFETERIA:

	MON	TUES	WED	THUR	FRI	SAT & SUN
B	cereal	toast	cereal	toast	cereal	toast + cereal!
L	pb & j sandwich	cheese sandwich	pb & j sandwich	cheese sandwich	pb & j sandwich	pb & j & cheese sandwich!
D	pasta with clam sauce	shiitake souffle	veggie burritos	cheese 'n' noodles	carob casserole	cha-cha chili & crackers

16

From the Horse's Mouth
BARBIE Q. ROAST

Tuesday

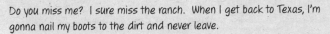

UNOPENED
OUTGOING MAIL
Forward to Lyle for Incineration

Chuck Roast
Chuck Roast Ranch
Porterhouse, Texas

Hey, Big Daddy!

Do you miss me? I sure miss the ranch. When I get back to Texas, I'm gonna nail my boots to the dirt and never leave.

You should see the lousy cabins they've got us living in. These rooms are smaller than the horse stalls in our barn!

Speaking of barns, would you believe these Harmony dames are making me clean out the stables here every day? I hope they're paying you big money for working me like a stock dog.

I'm bunking with two other gals. One's a real fancy pants sissy named Mimi. Guess what she calls my blue jeans? Dungarees! Not that she has any. She's never worn 'em. Have you ever heard such buffalo chips? She's from London, England — only she says it like this: "Lawn-don, Aing-lawnd." Instead of saying "very," she says "veddy." And everything's "luuuuhhhvely" this and "luuuuhhhvely" that. I told her to save some of her dadblamed luu-uuhhhvely breath for breathing.

The other gal in my cabin is a skinny thing named Charlotte. Quiet as a dead possum, but she's a pretty good dancer. Guess that's what the critters do up in Stopsign, Illinois.

I reckon the only thing I like about this dadgum place is that for four weeks, I'll be a whole lake away from Brisket (that rotten rump roast). Yee Haw!

Your favorite kid (I am, ain't I?),

- Barbie Q.

MIMI GEMS

UNOPENED

OUTGOING MAIL

Forward to Lyle for Incineration

3 July

Ms. Jewely Gems
Guest, Hôtel Magnifique
Paris, France

Dearest Mummy,

I hope you arrived safely in Paris. I'm fine, though I think you would be disappointed with the accommodations here at Camp Happy Harmony. Rather dismal, I'm afraid. (See sketch below.)

The other girls in my bungalow are, shall we say, not up to Good Egg Academy standards. Charlotte Lee, who comes from a small town in Illinois, has never been to Europe. (Can you imagine?) My other cottage-mate is a girl from Texas named Barbie O. Roast. She put steak sauce on her cereal yesterday morning — positively gruesome!

At least the King of Gruesome, Ivan the Horrible, is out of my sight. Kisses to you for that!

Cheerio, Mum!
Mimi

Here's where I sleep.

Barbie O. sleeps here.

This is Charlotte's bed.

I've seen mice here and here and here and here.

P.S. When I told the Harmony sisters how much I adore painting, they assigned me the task of renovating the Wisteria Cafeteria. I'm using a palette of cool melon shades. I do hope they like it.

Mr. and Mrs. Lee
Rural Route 1, Box 257
Stopsign, Illinois

Dear Mom and Dad,

Hi! How are you? Hope everything's OK at home.

It's just after dinner on our second full day of camp. We woke up this morning at 5:30(!) to the sound of the Harmonys singing "Good Morning, Sweet Sibling" on the loudspeaker.

No offense, but I can't believe you guys listened to this stuff when you were my age. And you think I have bad taste in music? Luckily, my roommates and I pretty much like the same kind of songs. I've been teaching them how to do the Flig. I can't believe how few dances they know. I guess Stopsign isn't as behind the times as I thought.

The schedule here is pretty rough. We do chores almost all day. You didn't tell me about *that* part. No wonder they call this place the camp that works! When we're not working, we have to go to cornball classes like Fishing For Compliments. (Ugh!)

And about these Harmony sisters . . . . Well, let's just say you'd have to see them to believe them. Darlene (she's the youngest sister) has apricot-colored hair and wears the goofiest clothes you've ever seen in your life. Dolly is the middle sister and the cook here. She must like her own cooking because her hands are the size of hams and her face is real puffy and shiny, like a glazed doughnut. (I feel kind of sorry for her.) The oldest sister, Dorothy, wears way too much perfume and has thin little eyebrows like a clown.

My roommates and I have to go to Bedtime Tantrums class tonight. I think I know why. One of the girls here (Mimi Gems) wanted to stay up really late last night. She threw a fit when the Harmony sisters turned the lights out at 9 o'clock. Dolly Harmony came in and gave her a cup of tea. When Dolly wasn't looking, Mimi threw it out the window. Then Dolly sang a corny little song called "Tea Is Like Sleep, So Let Your Dreams Steep." I couldn't help thinking of Charlie. He will absolutely DIE if they start singing these sappy songs to him!

Well, I better run. I've got to clean out the chicken coop before class.

Love you (but not this corny Harmony music or these chores) and miss you (but not Charlie),

Charlotte

P.S. Guess how many kids are enrolled at Camp Happy Harmony? Six! And that includes Charlie and me. (Big woo.) Guess the Harmonys aren't as popular as you -- or they -- thought!

OUTGOING MAIL

Forward to Lyle for Incineration

UNOPENED

WARDROBE ABODE
Fashions by Darlene

Dorothy,

I picked up the girls' letters from the mailbox, just like you said. Here's the form letter you asked me to write. Just forge the names of the girls on the last line and enclose a photo.

Toodles!

Darlene

P.S. I'll put any incoming mail to the kids in the recycling bin, right?

DOROTHY APPROVED

Dear (<u>insert parental reference here</u>),

Hi! How are you? I couldn't be better. Camp Happy Harmony is the greatest! Thanks so much for letting me spend my summer here!

The Harmony sisters are so much fun. And pretty, too! ~~Darlene~~ *Dorothy* is my favorite sister. She's nice, smart, beautiful AND talented. It's really an inspiration for me to see how she gets along so well with her brothers and sisters. Maybe after a month here, I'll be as kind and understanding as she is. I'm already starting to miss (<u>insert brother's name here</u>) a little bit.

Wish I had time to write more, but there are just so many exciting things to do here at Camp Happy Harmony! I hate to miss even a second of fun. Whatever you paid for me to attend this camp was really worth it!

I'll write again next week.

Love and miss you.

(<u>insert daughter's name here</u>)

I ♡ Camp Happy Harmony!

STAFF NOTE

Darlene and Dwayne,

A reminder to both of you: For security purposes, incoming mail should NOT be placed in the recycling bin.

Our standard operating procedure (and how many times do I have to remind you of this, Duh-rlene?) is that letters addressed to kids (from parents, etc.) should be delivered to Lyle's cabin for incineration.

Likewise, the kids' original letters home should be given to Lyle for destruction. I don't want any paper trails around here. Are you dummies clear on this?

Also, do not waste time or energy reading the letters the brats write home. And don't bother reading the incoming letters from parents either. You have work to do! Just pitch all letters in the barrel outside Lyle's cabin. He burns trash weekly.

Dwayne, let's have a POP HIT later tonight in the boys' bunks. Inspect the cabin for cleanliness and contraband materials.

Dorothy

 # SHARP NOTE #

During cabin inspection, various unapproved food items (chips, candy bars, pork rinds, etc.) were discovered under the bed of **Brisket Roast**. Because such foods are prohibited on camp grounds, they will be destroyed.

A duffle bag filled with compact discs and a travel stereo was confiscated from the locker of **Charlie Lee**. The recordings contained in the duffle bag were not those of The Harmony Family Singers. As this is a direct violation of Camp Happy Harmony regulations, the materials will be held in the Office of the Director until the end of session.

Dwayne Harmony
Dwayne Harmony

 CAMP-O-GRAM

Charlotte,

You're not going to believe this. We had a surprise cabin inspection last night. They called it a Pop Hit.

Dwayne Harmony took my travel stereo and all my CDs. He says the rule here is that we can't listen to any music except theirs. Is this cruel and unusual punishment, or what?

Anyway, I just wanted to warn you about Pop Hits. And I'm not telling you this to be nice. It's just that I don't want your CDs and headphones taken away, too. I may need to borrow them. Four weeks of this Harmony garbage is going to send me over the edge.

Charlie

TRANS-LAKE MAIL
- Delivered by Canoe -
Lyle Splink, Postmaster

CAMP-O-GRAM

Hi, Charlie.

Thanks for the heads up. And sorry to hear about Dwayne Harmony taking your CDs. But you think you've got it bad? Listen to this: Darlene Harmony replaced all the clothes I brought here (t-shirts, jeans, etc.) with the dorkiest dresses you've ever seen in your life! And we've got to wear this stuff for A WHOLE MONTH!

Do you know what chiffon is? It's that really fluffy material I used to wear in dance recitals a gazillion years ago. That's what these dresses are made of. And get a load of the colors: cotton candy pink, lime green and robin egg blue. I look like a walking Easter egg.

Poor Barbie Q.'s still crying. She's one of my room-mates. I guess she's never worn a dress before — ever! And certainly not one designed by Darlene Harmony. Are these Harmonys for real?

Charlotte

TRANS-LAKE MAIL
Delivered by Canoe
Lyle Splink, Postmaster

CAMP-O-GRAM

CHARLOTTE,

ARE THE HARMONYS FOR REAL? NO. I
THINK WE'RE BOTH JUST HAVING NIGHTMARES.
WAKE ME WHEN IT'S OVER.

UNTIL THEN, I'VE GOT AN IDEA. I'LL TRADE
YOU A PAIR OF MY JEANS FOR THREE OF YOUR
CDs — ASSUMING YOURS HAVEN'T BEEN CONFIS-
CATED YET. I SAW SOME CASSETTE AND CD
PLAYERS UP IN THE MELODY MANSION. IF I
WEAR HEADPHONES AND PRETEND I'M LISTENING
TO THAT SUGAR-COATED HARMONY JUNK, I CAN
HEAR SOME REAL MUSIC.

I'LL TRY TO HITCH A RIDE WITH LYLE ON THE
MAIL CANOE. IF YOU'RE GAME, MEET ME AT
THE BOAT DOCK TONIGHT AT 10:30 P.M. IF
YOU STILL HATE ME TOO MUCH TO MAKE THE
TRADE, I UNDERSTAND.

YOUR *DESPERATE* BROTHER,

CHARLIE

Charlie,

It's a deal. But you can't have my
Barfing Dogs CD. I'm teaching
Mimi and Barbie Q. to do the Flig
and I need the music.

See you at the dock.

Charlotte

26

 CAMP-O-GRAM

Hallo, Miss Lee.

   Allow me to introduce myself. My name is
Ivan Gems. I was born in London, England and
have lived there all my life, except for holi-
days. I am 13 years old and enjoy books on
every topic, but especially mysteries. I once
had a pet rabbit, since deceased, named
Sherlock.

   Your brother Charlie tells me you're teaching the girls* in your cabin the Flig. Would
you by any chance be willing to teach me, too?

   There's little doubt I look like a card-
carrying klutz. But in truth, I've been taking dance lessons since I was four years old.
The problem is, all the dances I learn in
London are the terribly dull ones, like the
waltz and the foxtrot. When it comes to dancing, I'm afraid I'm even less "cool," as you
Yankees say, than the Harmonys.

   I hope you'll not consider my request to
learn the Flig impertinent. I daresay my
social life would not be ill-served by the
experience. Chop chop!

   With the hope of one day making your
acquaintance,

                                    I am,

                              Ivan Gems

                              Ivan Gems

*including my reptilian sister Mimi

TRANS-LAKE MAIL
· Delivered by Canoe ·
Lyle Splink, Postmaster

CAMP-O-GRAM

Dear Ivan,

I'd be happy to teach you the Flig! It's really easy. And don't worry about being a klutz. My brother Charlie is the biggest knucklehead on the face of the earth. If he can do the Flig, anyone can -- including you.

Let's meet tonight after dinner in the ballroom of the Melody Mansion. That's where Barbie Q., Mimi and I like to dance — when we're not waxing the floors. (Who knew we were coming to a prison camp?)

Just hop a ride on the mail canoe. Charlie says Lyle's real nice about giving rides. Lyle's about the only normal adult here. Figures he's the only one who's not a Harmony.

See you tonight. Chop chop! (What does that mean, anyway?)

Charlotte Lee

P.S. You're wrong about ballroom dancing. Those old dances are really cool. I'd love to learn the foxtrot.

P.P.S. You're also wrong about your sister Mimi. I think she's a sweetie.

Here are the steps to the Flig:

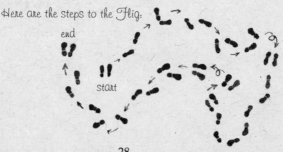

Dr. Dwayne Harmony
Nutritional Counselor

Hello, Dolly!

I finally got through to the record label. The producer,
Morrie Bigbucks, told me family acts are out. (As if we
hadn't noticed.) But he also said comebacks are very in,
especially for duos. And best of all, he agreed to listen to
our demo tape, "Duets by Dwayne and Dolly: Just the Two
of Us!"

Let's meet in the recording studio this week to finish up the
last two songs. I'd like to have something in the mail to
Bigbucks as soon as possible.

Of course, it bears repeating that no comeback will be possible until we resolve *the Lyle issue*. Can't you lean on
Dorothy to take care of that, once and for all?

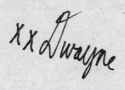

XX Dwayne

TRANS-LAKE MAIL
- Delivered by Canoe -
Lyle Splink, Postmaster

WISTERIA CAFETERIA

COOKIN' WITH DOLLY

Dwayney-kins,

Me? Lean on Dorothy?
Have you forgotten
The Wise One never listens
to anything I say? Here's a
replay of a conversation I had
with her earlier today:

Me: Dorothy, do you think it might be possible for
          Dwayne and me to sing a duet at the next
          camp sing-along?

Dorothy: No.

Me: Well, we have some new material we're work-
          ing on and —

Dorothy: I said no.

Me: Why?

Dorothy: Because I'm lead vocalist for The Harmony
          Family Singers, and I have a few solos I'd like
          to sing.

Me: Yeah, I bet you'd like to sing. Too bad you
          can't. Let's just wemember which of us is
          weally singing and which of us is just moving
          her wittle wips.

Dorothy: Very funny, Dogface. And let's also remember
          who's the smartest, the prettiest AND the boss
          around here. I said no duets at sing-alongs.
          End of conversation.

Yep, that's my sister for you. Charming, isn't she? Let me lean on
Darlene to lean on Dorothy. The fashion horse wants the Lyle problem taken care of so bad she can taste it.

I'll meet you at 8:30 Friday night in the recording studio. I've got to go
up there anyway to record some new material for Dorothy, the old
witch. I'll try to knock her stuff out fast so we'll have time to work on
our tape.

        XO Dolley

30

WARDROBE ABODE
Fashions by Darlene

Dorothy,

Dolly reminded me today that it's been 25 years since you
made that lousy deal with Lyle. You said then you'd think
of a way to get us out of it.

So, what gives? How much longer are you going to let Dale
and Daryl drag this thing out? With Lyle the Loser out of
the way, we can start planning The Harmony Family
Singers' comeback, AND (more importantly) I can launch
my line of designer clothes.

Besides, you promised I could have Lyle's cabin when he's
gone. I need it more than anyone since I have absolutely
zero closet space in this pitiful little Wardrobe Commode.

You're the boss. So make the twins do their job.

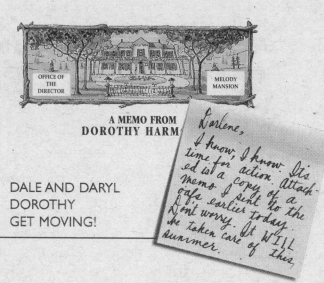

A MEMO FROM
DOROTHY HARM

Darlene,
I know, I know. It's time for action. Attached is a copy of a memo I sent to the oafs earlier today. Don't worry. It WILL be taken care of this summer.

TO: DALE AND DARYL
FR: DOROTHY
RE: GET MOVING!

Listen, you dolts: I thought we all agreed that this summer would be L's last. I don't want to know details. I just want it taken care of, the sooner, the better. The bills around here are getting harder and harder to keep up with. With L gone, we can sell this place and buy a top-of-the-line tour bus so we can take our show on the road again.

Pull up your socks and get moving. I want results. NOW!

Dorothy

STAFF NOTE

COPY

DA TWINS

Look, Doro. We're trying.

Our problem is Jazz, that scurvy
mutt. He yaps his fool head off
every time we get ~~klo~~ close to Lyle.
You lay one hand on Lyle and Jazz goes
nuts. And then with all these kids around
. . . . Well, we didn't think it was a good
idea to risk getting ~~caw~~ caught in the act.
Better wait till the kids are gone.

But why do we have to do the
dirty deed anyway? Can't
Dwayne do it? He's got all those
~~goremay~~ fancy recipes.
Can't he
just cook
Lyle something that'll knock his
socks off? (Ha!)

D and D

TRANS-LAKE MAIL
- Delivered by Canoe -
Lyle Splink, Postmaster

OFFICE OF THE DIRECTOR

MELODY MANSION

A MEMO FROM
DOROTHY HARMONY

STAFF NOTE

TO: DALE AND DARYL
FR: DOROTHY
RE: STUPID QUESTIONS

NO, you numskulls. You know Lyle won't eat any of Dwayne's food. He's a picky eater and always has been. (Don't you remember how Mom used to say Lyle was the fussiest eater she'd ever seen?)

Quit stalling. We've got bills up the kazoo to pay. And I want to put a down payment on a customized tour bus.

I'll get Dwayne to come up with something to take care of the dog. You two deal with Lyle.

Dorothy

P.S. You know darn well why you bozos have to do the dirty deed. You're the youngest and dumbest. So there.

P.P.S. And quit calling me Doro.

TRANS-LAKE MAIL
- Delivered by Canoe -
Lyle Splink, Postmaster

FROM THE DESK OF DOROTHY HARMONY

Dwayne,
Below are my observations about the rugrats. Please prescribe the appropriate nutritional remedies and tell Dolly to prepare evening meals in accordance. Also, Dale and Daryl are having difficulty dealing with L because of Jazz. Take care of the mutt.

NAME	AGE	PROBLEM	RECIPES
Ivan Gems	13	Reads too much	Eye strain chow mein
Mimi Gems	11½	Won't go to bed; stays up all night painting	Out-like-a-light tea
Brisket Roast	12	Slob; eats like there's no tomorrow	Put this kid on the "Canned and Bland" diet
Barbie Q. Roast	12	A real tomboy and a loud mouth	Spaghetti with clam-up clam sauce
Charlie Lee	12	Listens to rock 'n' roll; serious attitude problem	Lite rock pork chops
Charlotte Lee	11	I just don't like this kid	Formula #1222 + Hasta la pasta

Dr. Dwayne Harmony
Camp Happy Harmony
Harmony Hills, MO

Office Hours: By Appointment Only

NAME
ADDRESS Dorothy,

AGE
DATE

Rx I've suggested recipes and will forward to Dolly. Don't worry about the dog. I'll devise a recipe and have Dolly bake up a dog biscuit. Dale and Daryl can administer at their earliest convenience.

Dwayne

Refill ___ times
☐ Label

SUBSTITUTION PERMITTED

DISPENSE AS WRITTEN

FORM 1322

CONFIDENTIAL

♪ EF NOTE

We'd Rather Sing Than F...
'Cause Being Polite Is S...
(The Harmony Fam...

A HARMONIC NOTE FROM YOUR BROTHERS

Ivan, Charlie and Brisket:
Hi ya, fellas! Here's the sheet music for this week's sing-along. And don't forget: letters home are due Saturday.

Dwayne   Dale
Daryl

(Verses...

We're sib...
But unli...
We're s...
And we nev...

We don't fight; we don't curse.
We think bad manners are even worse.
We're well-behaved, as you can see.
We're one big happy family.

Because . . .

Refrain:
We'd rather sing than fight,
'Cause being polite is such a delight.
It may sound corny and trite,
But sibling joy is our birthright.

We cherish our siblings
'Cause they're our parents' offspring.
And we're a credit to our mother
When we love one another.

That's why we're always good as gold,
We do exactly as we're told.
When they write our biography
They'll say we're the perfect family!

Because . . .

(Repeat Refrain)

UNOPENED

Harmony Hills, Missouri
601 Melody Lane
Camp Happy Harmony

USA 32
HARMONY

Mr. and Mrs. Lee
Route 1, Box 257
Illinois

July 7

Dear Mom and Dad,

You guys must really hate your children to send us off to a camp like this. Did you know they'd take my CDs and replace them with The Harmony Family's Greatest Hits? Or that they'd take Charlotte's clothes and make her wear prom dresses all summer? They've got us boys wearing leisure suits!

And did you know they'd make us sing the all-time worst, corniest, most stupid songs ever written???

Last night when I snuck up to the Melody Mansion to listen to one of Charlotte's CDs, I heard the most ear-splitting sounds coming from the recording studio. Turns out it was Dolly and Dwayne Harmony singing a duet. The words they were singing were bad enough (something like "Love denied makes the turtle-doves cry"), but their voices were even worse. I'm making up my own lyrics to their song: "Songs so foul make hound dogs howl."

Well, I'm *trying* to be good, but it's not easy around here.

One week down, three more to go.

Love,
Charlie

From the Plate of
BRISKET ROAST

OUTGOING MAIL

Forward to Lyle for Incineration

ˋUNOPENEDˊ

Saturday

Chuck Roast
Chuck Wagon Ranch
Porterhouse, Texas

WHY'D YOU MAKE ME COME TO THIS STINKIN' SUM-
MER CAMP?

I know how you hate griping, Big Daddy, but tough toe-
nails. These Harmony yahoos have got me so mad, I'm
fixin' to spit REAL nails. They're working us half to
death, cleaning up this dump they call a camp. The cabins
are so cramped, you couldn't swing a stiff coyote without hitting a wall.

And if that don't yank your tail, the food here is worse
than the slop we feed the hogs. Dolly Harmony gave us
something today she tried to pass off as chili. Nice try!
It was weaker than soup made from the shadow of a
crow that starved to death.

What I'd give to teach these hillbillies how to cook real chili,
the kind that makes your eyeballs sweat. Now THAT'S good
eatin'.

So how about sendin' me a few provisions? The dang
Harmonys stole my other grub before I even got a
taste of your homemade pork rinds. It's just not
fair. Why'd you send me to this dadgum camp in the
first place?

I reckon I might consider forgivin' you if you send me
some hot sauce, jerky and chips. Salsa, too. And some
corn bread and buttermilk. Grits? A slab of bacon
maybe?

Hungrier than the hills,

Brisket

Ivan Gems

⌐UNOPENED⌐

7 July

Ms. Jewely Gems
Guest, Hôtel Magnifique
Paris, France

Hallo, Mummy.

I do hope you're well. Life here at
Camp Happy Harmony is . . . well, the word
"intriguing" comes to mind. I think you
would find The Harmony Family Singers most
amusing.

For all the talk about what wonderful
friends the Harmony siblings are, you'd
never know it to see them in person. The
brothers barely speak to one another.
More often than not, they shoot each other
dirty looks with eyes that glisten like
daggers. An unmistakable odor of oddness
clings to the three men; something doesn't
quite ring true.

I've only seen the three Harmony sisters
from a distance, but the oldest sister,
Dorothy, has a voice like a freight train.
She is forever yelling at middle sister
Dolly, who always stomps off in a huff,
and at Darlene, the youngest and perhaps
dimmest sister. Instead of Camp Happy
Harmony, they should call this operation
Camp Cacophony.

Fortunately, the campers here are far more harmonious in temperament. One of the girls (Charlotte) is teaching me how to dance the Flig. Don't worry, Mummy. We're also ballroom dancing. I'm teaching the girls how to waltz and foxtrot. The boys show no interest in dancing.

I meet the girls on the sly, which isn't nearly as difficult as you might imagine. Lyle Splink, the Harmonys' former bus driver, told me the Harmonys are asleep most nights by nine o'clock. So at that hour, I creep quietly down to the dock and wait for Lyle, who gives me rides across the lake in his mail canoe.

When the moon is reflected in the lake, it feels magical and mysterious, like something out of a novel. I mentioned this to Lyle last night. He replied, rather sadly: "You sure could write a book about this place."

I wonder what he meant.

From America,

OUTGOING MAIL

Forward to Lyle for Incineration

OFFICIAL LETTER HOME
WEEK I/BOYS

[DOROTHY APPROVED]

Dear (<u>insert parental reference here</u>)

Hi! How are you?

I'm great! You would the boys' original letters home and
Harmony is. The H replaced them with our form letter.
are SO cool. The f I'll attach a copy for your file. I
music is the best! dropped off originals, plus all incoming mail to kids, at Lyle's cabin for
Thanks so much f incineration.
Harmony!

Doro,

As per your request, I've collected
the boys' original letters home and
replaced them with our form letter.
I'll attach a copy for your file. I
dropped off originals, plus all incoming mail to kids, at Lyle's cabin for
incineration.

Later, "sis."

Dwayne

Your son,

(insert son's name here)

Boy, am I having fun!

41

Howdy, Barbie Q. and Brisket!

How the sam hog are you two? Hope it's going right as rain up there in the Ozarks. Things down here aren't the same without you. Heck, I'm not gonna get all corn mushy about it. Let's just say it's like eating ribs without slaw. Just doesn't feel right.

Speaking of ribs and slaw, I'm sending you each ('cause I know you can't share worth a pig's eye) a bodacious care package of vittles to supplement the camp chow. Give me a holler when you run out.

Love and all that chicken-fried sentimental stuff,

Big Daddy

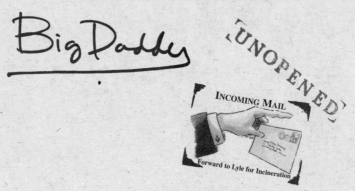

Have you tried our famous beef jerky ice cream?

Rural Route 1, Box 257
Stopsign, Illinois

Dear Charlotte and Charlie,

We knew you'd like the Harmonys once you got to meet them in person!

After you left, we dug out all our old Harmony Family Singers' posters and albums. Won't it be terrific when we can listen to their music together as one big happy family?

We love and miss you both.

Mom and Dad

P.S. Please share these cookies with your new friends, the Harmonys!

43

LA TOUR EIFFEL (1887-1889) PARIS

Mes cheris,

I'm so pleased to hear you're enjoying Camp Happy Harmony.

It gave me no pleasure to send you there against your will, but I simply couldn't bear another summer of your constant bickering. Nor could I allow you, Ivan, to waste away another summer reading those silly mysteries. (You know your Auntie Moira calls them "literature for the lowbrow.") And, Mimi, if your grandparents knew you wanted to be an artist (a watercolourist, no less!), your trust fund would disappear overnight.

I do miss you. But I truly believe some rigorous outdoor exercise will do you both a world of good. Furthermore, I have every confidence that time spent with the ever-loving Harmony family will give you a greater respect for the institution of family, especially the precious Gem family.

With kisses to you both,
I am always,
Your Mum

RÉPUBLIQUE FRANÇAISE

POSTES 3.20

PARIS HARMONIE
7 Juillet
FRANCE

PAR AVION
AIR MAIL

Mimi and Ivan Gems

Camp Happy Harmony

601 Melody Lane

Harmony Hills, Missouri

USA

INCOMING MAIL

Forward to Lyle for Incineration

44

THINGS TO DO THIS WEEK:

☐ Call Beautiful Buses. Discuss my ideas for customizing bus. Send first payment.

☐ Call 1st Ozark Country Meadow Bank. Discuss short-term loan options. Tell them we'll have $$$ as soon as we sell camp.

☐ Find out what's taking the twins so long to deal with L.

☐ Have Dolly record new songs for me to sing at this week's sing-along.

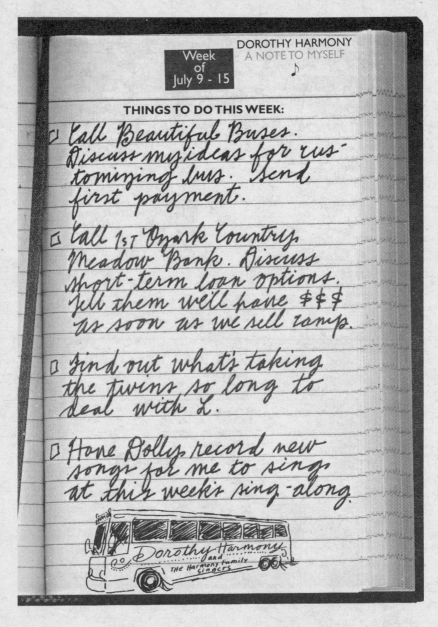

46

CAMP HAPPY HARMONY LEDGER

Week of July 9 - 15

DATE	DESCRIPTION	✓	+ INCOME	− EXPENSES
7/10	Royalties		27.98	
7/12	My speaking fee (american association of Retired singers)		100.00	
7/13	Pawn Darlene's tiara collection		179.00	
			306.98	
7/9	Director's salary			2,000.00
7/15	Other staff salary			1,000.00
7/13	First payment on bus			12,000.00
7/13	Groceries (for us)			459.55
7/14	Groceries (for kids)			24.25
7/15	Miscellaneous expenses			369.00
				15,852.80

Weekly Balance: −$15,545.82
Last Week's Balance: 2,464.11
Current Balance: −$13,081.71

PAWN PALACE
43 faux-diamond tiaras:
$179

Gourmet Goodies
Fabulous Food for Fabulous People

baby corn relish
fresh crabmeat
roasted red peppers
pesto pasta
tangerine sorbet
dark chocolate fudge sauce (lots)
gourmet vanilla ice cream

TOTAL: $459.55
DELIVER TO CAMP HAPPY HARMONY
(back entrance) — C/O DOROTHY

BEAUTY HUT
The Ozarks' House of Beauty

Client Name:
Dorothy Harmony

hair analysis
consultation
hair plugs
Fee: $369.00

SAVE-MORE WHOLESALE FOODS
Damaged and Dented
But Still Pretty OK Groceries

bulgur .... 2@2.09
bread (week old) .... 3@.99
surplus peanut butter 2.09
rutabagas 2.99
instant potatoes 2.09
dehydrated onion flakes .... 5@.89
.... 2@1.69
COST : $24.25

PAYMENT #1: $12,000.00

WEEK TWO
CLASS SCHEDULE

SISTERS	BROTHERS

Monday

The Art of Vacuuming	Weeding Is Fun!
Instructor: Darlene	Instructor: Dwayne
Place: Melody Mansion	Place: Organic garden

Tuesday

Let's Clean Closets!	Elocution, Elocution, Elocution
Instructor: Darlene	Instructor: Dwayne
Place: Wardrobe Abode	Place: Melody Mansion

Wednesday

Kettles and Pots and Pans - OH MY!	How to Whistle As You Work
Instructor: Dolly	Instructor: Daryl
Place: Wisteria Cafeteria	Place: Stables
Letters home due today	

Thursday

Sing-Along with the Harmony Sisters	Wilderness Skills
Instructor: Dorothy	Instructor: Daryl
Place: Melody Mansion	Place: Nature Trails

Friday

BeBop As You Slop (Pigs)	Singing for Health
Instructor: Darlene	Instructor: Dwayne
Place: Pig pen	Place: Melody Mansion

Saturday

Wilderness Skills	Let's Paint Fences
Instructor: Dolly	Instructor: Dale
Place: Nature Trails	Place: Meet in
	Wisteria Cafeteria
	Letters home due today

Sunday

Rest and Relaxation	Rest and Relaxation
All Camp Evening Sing-Along	All Camp Evening Sing-Along

ACTIVITIES
WEEK TWO

GIRLS	BOYS
continue renovating cafeteria	stack hay bales in barn
gather eggs; milk goats (twice/day)	break rocks in quarry
wash dishes (all meals)	feed pigs (twice/day)
brush burros	dust administrative offices
vacuum all camp buildings	weed vegetable garden
scour all kettles/pots/pans	wash all windows
re-sod lawn in front of Melody Mansion	patch cracked plaster (all buildings)
write one letter home	write one letter home

WEATHER FORECAST:
Hot and sunny all week. No chance of rain. Drought advisory posted for all counties in southern Missouri. No-burn order in effect for entire Ozark region. Camp fires and burn piles prohibited.

THIS WEEK AT THE WISTERIA CAFETERIA:

	MON	TUES	WED	THUR	FRI	SAT & SUN
B	toast	toast	cereal	toast	cereal	toast + cereal!
L	pb & j sandwich	cheese sandwich	pb & j sandwich	cheese sandwich	pb & j sandwich	toast + cereal!
D	Each camper will be served an evening meal custom-prepared by Chef Dolly with recipes developed by nutritional counselor Dr. Dwayne Harmony. Bon appetit!					pb & j & cheese sandwich!

CAMP-O-GRAM

Hey, Charlie.

You don't know me from Eve, but I wanted to holler a big old Texas-sized THANK YOU to your side of the lake.

I'm bunking over here with your sister Charlotte. She lent me a pair of your blue jeans to wear when the Harmony sisters aren't giving us the hairy eyeball. If I'd known these dadgum broads were gonna make me wear long dresses every day, I never would have come to this sissified camp!

Anyway, Charlotte told me about the swap. Now don't worry your warts off, Chuck. I won't spill the beans. And I'll return your jeans at the end of camp.

- Barbie Q. Roast

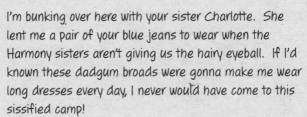

P.S. I think you're bunking with my meathead brother Brisket. Don't hold it against me, Hoss.

49

CAMP·O·GRAM

Hi, Barbie Q.

Glad to be of service with the jeans.

Are you the girl I saw on Sunday riding the horse named Sadie around the Melody Mansion? I thought I recognized my jeans. Would you by any chance be willing to teach me how to ride? If so, the jeans are yours to keep.

Charlie

P.S. Brisket's great! We all like him over here. He's waiting on a care package of food from your dad. He says he's going to fix us a feast that'll put this Harmony chow to shame. Can't wait!

P.P.S. I feel sorry for you having to bunk with my noodlehead sister Charlotte.

TRANS-LAKE MAIL
- Delivered by Canoe -
Lyle Splink, Postmaster

CAMP·O·GRAM

Hey again, Charlie!

Jeans for riding lessons? Sounds fair and square to me. After supper tonight, I'll hitch a ride over to your side of the lake with Lyle. He lets me wear my cowboy hat in his canoe.

And just so you know — Sadie's a burro, not a horse. And Charlotte is NOT a noodlehead. I don't give a rat's rump if she is your sister. You sass my friend again and I'll make sure I find you a burro who likes to do his business on your boots.

Meet me at the stables. And I've got first dibs on Sadie. She's the fastest burro they've got.

- Barbie Q.

P.S. I can spit 50 yards and blow my nose without a handkerchief. I'd be willing to teach you these tricks, too, if you'll swap me for another pair of blue jeans. Think about it, kid.

TRANS-LAKE MAIL
· Delivered by Canoe ·
Lyle Splink, Postmaster

CAMP-O-GRAM

Dear Mister Brisket Roast,

Forgive my forwardness, but my new friend (and your twin) Barbie Q. tells me you've requested food from home and are planning a secret dinner for the boys.

Would you think it horribly rude of me if I invited myself, along with Barbie Q. and Charlotte, to your banquet? The food here is so atrocious, I fear we shall all perish from starvation.

I would be happy to help with the meal in any way I can. I'm not much of a cook, but I do have some lovely Belgian chocolates I'd be delighted to donate to the cause. Maybe I could melt the chocolates and make some tarts or a cake. Perhaps even a chocolate mousse? May I borrow a recipe?

Yours in the culinary arts,

Mimi Gems

Also, Mr. Roast: I pity the fact you have to share close quarters with my brother Ivan. I don't suppose we could exclude him from the dinner party, could we?

TRANS-LAKE MAIL
- Delivered by Canoe -
Lyle Splink, Postmaster

Howdy-do, Miss Mimi!

Heck yes, you can help with the supper I'm fixin' to make! That is, as soon as my supplies arrive. My daddy must've sent the grub by pony express.

You've got chocolate? I love chocolate. But recipes? I never use 'em. I cook by ear, eye, nose, and of course, mouth.

But if you want a recipe, they've got plenty of cookbooks over in the "Bacteria cafeteria," as your brother Ivan calls it. I'll sneak over and sniff out a recipe for a chocolate dessert you can make.

Nice to meet ya, Miss Mimi!

Brisket

P.S. What's wrong with Ivan? He's my compadre. Now if you want to un-invite my sister Barbie Q., that's none of my funeral.

P.P.S. One other thing. I'd be obliged if you'd call me just plain Brisket. Mr. Roast is my daddy.

TRANS-LAKE MAIL
- Delivered by Canoe -
Lyle Splink, Postmaster

We'd Rather Sing Than Fight,
'Cause Being Polite Is Such A Delight

(The Harmony Family Theme Song)

(Verses III and IV — sisters only)

As sisters not brothers,
We're unlike the others.
Our goal is no mystery:
It's to be kind and so sisterly.

We're like angels without wings;
You may call us sweet things.
Hark and hear the bells ring
When we join hands to sing:

Refrain

From sisters and daughters
Flow love like rainwaters.
We're the flowers that bloom,
And the smell of perfume.

We're clean and we're pretty;
We're soft as a kitty.
And we look like sweet princesses
When we wear our neat chintz dresse̶s̶

A Hi Note from Darlene
The darling sister says...

Hi, Girls!

Tomorrow night is sing-along with the Harmony sisters. We'll be singing verses three and four of "We'd Rather Sing Than Fight, 'Cause Being Polite Is Such A Delight." Your parents will be so tickled when they hear you perform this Harmony favorite on Sibling Appreciation Day!

Speaking of which, we want to keep Camp Happy Harmony looking shipshape. Let's vacuum the carpets in all buildings mornings AND evenings this week, okey dokey? I've got some adorable scarves for you to wear while you clean. You know what we Harmony sisters say: *Cleaning in style makes everyone smile!*

Don't forget: letters home are due today.

Smiles!

Darlene

54

Mr. and Mrs. Lee
Rural Route 1, Box 257
Stopsign, Illinois

Dear Mom and Dad,

OK, you two, tell it to me straight. Am I adopted?

There's no way I am genetically related to anyone who actually likes these dumb Harmony songs. It's just not possible. Or did everyone back then listen to this kind of sappy music?

Luckily, my two roommates aren't saps at all. They're really cool. Mimi is giving me art lessons. And Barbie Q. is an incredible trick rider. She's teaching Mimi and me how to ride burros — standing up! I'm teaching them and a boy named Ivan how to dance the Flig.

Better sign off now. I've got to lay sod on two acres tonight. Did you know they'd work us half to death here?

Love,

Charlotte

P.S. Since I have to write home once a week, I think you guys should have to write back. So far I haven't received a single letter from home. I thought you said you'd write to Charlie and me every week. What's up?

MIMI GEMS

Ms. Jewely Gems
Guest, Hôtel Magnifique
Paris, France

UNOPENED

Dear Mumsley,

DO ignore my previous letter to you regarding my cottagemates. I am positively enchanted with them. We keep one another in stitches with our imitations of the Harmony sisters, who are absolute slave drivers AND mad as hatters, all of them.

Yesterday we finished painting the cafeteria. Now the sisters want us to paint the theater in the Melody Mansion. I have in mind a mural project.

Wish I had more time to write, but the girls and I must get back to work. Today we're pushing around a trio of horribly noisy contraptions known as *vacuums.* Imagine!

Adieu for now.

Mimi

Barbie Q.

Me

Charlotte

From the Horse's Mouth
BARBIE Q. ROAST

Wednesday

Chuck Roast
Chuck Wagon Ranch
Porterhouse, Texas

Big Daddy,

I'm not sure I'm even talking to you!

My bunkmates and me had to get up at 4:30 this morning to collect eggs for breakfast. And we didn't even get to eat the dang things. We got cream of bulgur cereal (tastes like burnt tractor tires) while the slick-eared Harmonys scarfed down humongous omelets. Then, after breakfast, Mimi, Charlotte and I had to wash our dishes PLUS theirs (which were all crusty with eggs) and scrub all the pots and pans.

And you should see the clothes these Harmony dames have got us wearing. I'm not kidding, Big Daddy. These dresses are uglier than a pimple on a possum. Lucky for me Charlotte loaned me a pair of her brother's jeans to wear when the Harmony broads are getting their beauty sleep. That's when us kids and our pal Lyle throw ourselves a nightly shindig to beat the band.

But just 'cause I'm making the best of a bad situation doesn't excuse you for sending me here. You've got some explaining to do, Big Daddy.

- Barbie Q.

OFFICIAL LETTER HOME
WEEK 2/GIRLS

DOROTHY APPROVED!

Dear (<u>insert parental reference here</u>),

Wow! My second week at Camp Happy Harmony is shaping up to be even more fun than the first!

I'm learning so much from the Harmony sisters. They're teaching me how to be a sweet sister to (<u>insert brother's name here</u>). Plus, I've been swimming, hiking, canoeing, burro-back riding, singing and lots more!

Life on a farm is SO ~~ ~~ wish I could stay ALL
~~ ~~ weeks.

Dorothy,
I delivered the girls' letters to Lyle for incineration. Here's the form letter to send to the parents. Just forge each girl's name on the last line and enclose a photo.

By the way, isn't it about time for a POP HIT on our side of the lake?

Darlene

This is the best camp EVER!

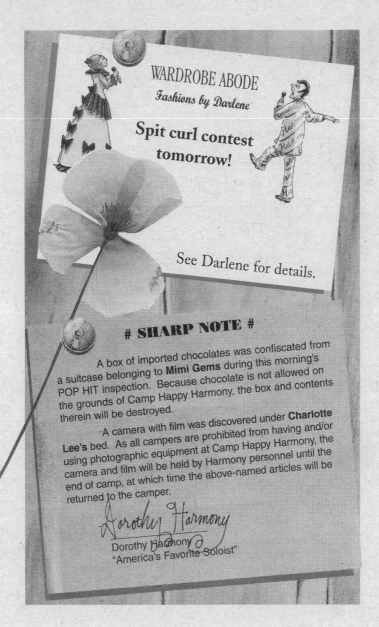

WARDROBE ABODE

Fashions by Darlene

Spit curl contest tomorrow!

See Darlene for details.

SHARP NOTE

A box of imported chocolates was confiscated from a suitcase belonging to **Mimi Gems** during this morning's POP HIT inspection. Because chocolate is not allowed on the grounds of Camp Happy Harmony, the box and contents therein will be destroyed.

A camera with film was discovered under **Charlotte Lee's** bed. As all campers are prohibited from having and/or using photographic equipment at Camp Happy Harmony, the camera and film will be held by Harmony personnel until the end of camp, at which time the above-named articles will be returned to the camper.

Dorothy Harmony
"America's Favorite Soloist"

Dearest Brisket,

Remember the Belgian chocolates I offered for the outlaw feast? Well, they were stolen this morning by those horrible Harmony sisters. Poor Charlotte lost her camera in the heist.

May I still help plan the secret dinner soiree, even though I have nothing to add to the pot, so to speak?

Chocolate-less on this side of the lake,

Mimi

TRANS-LAKE MAIL
- Delivered by Canoe -
Lyle Splink, Postmaster

Miss Mimi,

Are you pullin' my tail? Of course you can still help with the supper! Why don't you design the invitations? Ivan says you're a real good artist.

And don't worry about the chocolates being wrangled. I snuck into the Bacteria cafeteria last night after lights out. I couldn't find any recipes for chocolate desserts anyway. Only carob crud.

But here's what I couldn't figure. Now I don't pretend to know much about cookbooks, but aren't recipes usually divided into categories like this?

Soups
Breads
Salads
Meats
Desserts

The reason I ask is because the recipes in Dolly Harmony's files were divided into stuff like this.

Bed wetters
Brats
Loud mouths
Pain in the necks
Up-all-nighters

There were more than that, but I can't remember the rest. Weird as worms, hey?

Anyhoo, I'm looking forward to our outlaw chow. Of course all this planning may be for nothing, considering I still haven't gotten my dadburn care package yet from my daddy. I'll holler your way when my supplies arrive.

Brisket

CAMP-O-GRAM

Ivan, Charlie and Brisket:

Listen up, fellas. Serious stuff. The three of us snuck into the Bacteria Cafeteria last night after a tip from Brisket. And get this — them Harmony weasels have got files on each of us!

In Mimi's file it said she stays up all night. Then there was this recipe for something called "Out-Like-A-Light Tea." This must be what Dolly gives Mimi every night —

And which I promptly toss out the window of our cottage! Ivan, there was a note in your file about reading too much. The recommended "remedy" was something called "Eye Strain Chow Mein." Was that not the ghastly dinner Dolly served you Monday night, and which you claimed was completely inedible? (Thank goodness!)

We don't know about y'all, but we're not buying this pony. The good thing is that dinner looks like the only contaminated meal, meaning breakfast and lunch are OK.

We still have to show up for dinner. But we don't have to eat this junk. Just push it around on your plate. Bury the big stuff under the lettuce leaves. Throw the other gunk in your milk.

But here's a happy notion: There's an abundance of fruit in the orchard and vegetables in the garden. We can gather eggs from the chicken house and milk from the goats. Charlotte, Barbie Q. and I will prepare our evening meal tonight over a campfire in the apple orchard. Would you boys care to join us? If so, meet us in the orchard at 9:30, after lights out.

Mimi   - Barbie Q.   Charlotte

This is just one of the recipes we found in Dolly's recipe box. It was filed under "Deadly Dinners."   ------------>

The Ozark Mountain Mushroom

The poisonous variety of this spore does not occur naturally. However, given proper greenhouse conditions, this naughty mushroom can be cultivated and grown indoors with great success.

But be careful, gentle reader. The Ozark Mountain mushroom is truly the deadliest mushroom of all. Save it and the following recipe for your most ambitious (ho ho!) projects.

Mushroom Stroganoff   (Serves 6)

Prepare the sauce of this savory stroganoff in advance and store in the refrigerator or freezer. Thaw four hours before serving.

1 cup goat milk	1 Tbsp. fresh (salted)
1 Tbsp. cornstarch	1 small onion
2 cups Ozark	2 cloves garlic, minced
Mountain mushrooms	1/3 cup Formula LTVZ
(poisonous), sliced	salt and pepper to taste

Combine goat milk and cornstarch and set aside onion and garlic in butter. Stir in mushrooms and LTVZ. When tender, remove mushrooms and juices the pan and add the goat milk mixture. Cook until thickened. Return mushrooms and juices to pan. Serve over noodles or rice. And don't forget to call the funeral home.

Chapter Seven: Oh, You Naughty Mushroom!

 # CAMP-O-GRAM

To Mimi, Charlotte and Barbie Q.:

Deadly dinners?? Funeral home???
No thanks, cowpokes!

YOUR PLAN SOUNDS GOOD. WE'LL BE THERE.
IN THE MEANTIME, I'LL TRY TO GET THROUGH
TO OUR PARENTS ON THE TELEPHONE.

With heart-felt thanks for your kind
invitation,

We are,

Your devoted campmates,

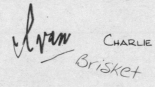 CHARLIE
Brisket

TRANS-LAKE MAIL
- Delivered by Canoe -
Lyle Splink, Postmaster

P.S. Maybe we could take turns. You
gals make supper tonight. We'll cook
tomorrow night.

P.P.S. IS IT OK IF WE INVITE LYLE TO DIN-
NER? HE'S BEEN REAL NICE ABOUT GIVING US
RIDES IN HIS CANOE. BESIDES, HE ALWAYS
EATS ALONE IN HIS CABIN WITH JUST HIS DOG
FOR COMPANY.

P.P.P.S. And who can blame Lyle?
Given his choice of dining companions
(the Harmonys vs. his dog), I say the
old boy shows good judgment.

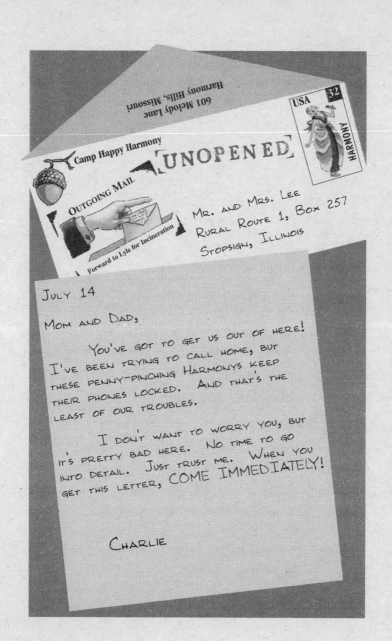

601 Melody Lane
Harmony Hills, Missouri

USA 32
HARMONY

Camp Happy Harmony
UNOPENED

OUTGOING MAIL

Forward to Lyle for Incineration

Mr. and Mrs. Lee
Rural Route 1, Box 257
Stopsign, Illinois

July 14

Mom and Dad,

You've got to get us out of here!
I've been trying to call home, but
these penny-pinching Harmonys keep
their phones locked. And that's the
least of our troubles.

I don't want to worry you, but
it's pretty bad here. No time to go
into detail. Just trust me. When you
get this letter, COME IMMEDIATELY!

Charlie

From the Plate of **UNOPENED**
BRISKET ROAST

Now look-a-here, Big Daddy.

Are you sendin' me my chow or what? I need the grub so I can fix my compadres some real food - - not like the poisoned slop they've got here. That's right, Big Daddy. POISONED SLOP! That's what these good-for-nothing Harmonys have been trying to feed us for supper.

We don't eat it, of course. I'm head chef of the hush-hush cookouts we have every night after lights out. Last night I made pan-fried catfish from a whole mess of fish Barbie Q. caught using crickets for bait. Everybody said it was the best chow they'd had since we got here. (The catfish, I mean. Not the crickets.)

Lyle loaned me his grill and some skillets. He says we shouldn't build a campfire like the girls did 'cause it's too dangerous. It hasn't rained worth spit here in three weeks and no one's supposed to burn anything 'cause of the risk of fire. Heck, charcoal and a grill are OK by me. I've only been barbecuing since I was in diapers!

So I've been feeding seven mouths every night for supper. Make that 7 1/2 mouths, including Jazz. (That's Lyle's dog.) I haven't eaten any red meat all week. I may become one of those vegetarians you're always cussing about.

But I need some seasonings, Daddy. So please send me the grub I asked for. Then git your gittyup in gear and come git us out of this dad-blamed death trap!

Your starvin' son,
Brisket

Ivan Gems

⌐UNOPENED⌐

14 July

Ms. Jewely Gems
Guest, Hôtel Magnifique
Paris, France

My dear Mum,

What a difference a week makes.

It seems like just yesterday I was writing to
you about dance lessons. Well, I'm still dancing --
and so are my roommates, who were intrigued by my
nocturnal adventures.

Last night after dining together in the orchard,
the six of us (Mimi, Charlotte, Barbie Q., Brisket,
Charlie and I) met in secret in the old barn. Our
friend Lyle showed us a huge room on the second
floor where farmers once stored hay. Now it's our
dance hall. And Lyle is our disc jockey!

Charlotte hid her portable stereo in the barn so
the Harmony sisters couldn't confiscate it. Such
pluck, that Charlotte! But frankly, even if the
Harmonys did find our musical stash, I expect we'd
still have fun. Charlie (that's Charlotte's brother) is a wonderful entertainer. His parodies of
the Harmonys, especially their singing, are most
comical. And I'm actually getting quite proficient
at doing the Flig. Even Mimi danced with me once
last night.

Oh, there is one tiny lump in the oatmeal. We
think the Harmonys may be trying to poison us.
Don't fret, Mum. We've all pledged not to touch
the vile dinners prepared by Dolly Harmony.

I do hope you're enjoying your vacation, as well
as my weekly updates of this most unusual adventure.

Yours dramatically,

Ivan i

OUTGOING MAIL

Forward to Lyle for Incineration

67

OFFICIAL LETTER HOME
WEEK 2/BOYS

DOROTHY APPROVED

Dear (<u>insert parental reference here</u>),

Gosh! Camp Happy Harmony just gets more exciting by the minute!

I've been swimming, fishing and canoeing every day with the Harmony brothers, who are the greatest guys in the whole world! I especially like how they treat me just like one of their brothers. What an honor!

See you at Sibling Appre

Your son,

(insert son's name her

Dorothy,

I've forwarded the boys' original letters home, as well as all incoming mail, to Lyle for incineration.

Here are photos and form letter #2 to send to the parents. *Dwayne*

I want to spend EVERY summer here!

No Meal Is Complete Without A Little Red Meat

Hi-ho, Barbie Q. and Brisket!

I'm tickled pinker than a piglet that y'all are enjoying your-
selves up there at that camp. 'Course that bit about wishing
you could stay all summer, Barbie Q., kinda hurt my feelings. But I reckon you're both just growing up. One of
these days you'll ride off into the sunset and leave old Big
Daddy here by his lonesome.

Until then, I'm sending along another round of care packages. I reckon they're feeding you real fine up there, but
you can't beat the eats we got down here in the Lone Star
state. So enjoy the grub and holler when you need more.

Love con carne,

Big Daddy

Put some steak on your pancakes!

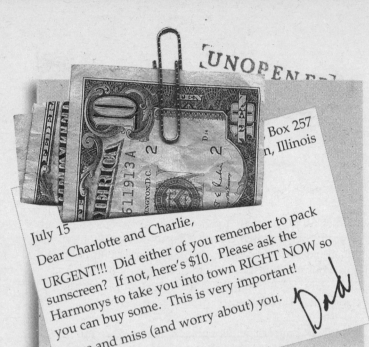

UNOPENED

Box 257
n, Illinois

July 15

Dear Charlotte and Charlie,

URGENT!!! Did either of you remember to pack sunscreen? If not, here's $10. Please ask the Harmonys to take you into town RIGHT NOW so you can buy some. This is very important!

I love and miss (and worry about) you.

Dad

the Harmonys' music once
y.... ...our dad and I are listening to their
alb... ...all the time now. We dug out all our old Harmony family memorabilia from the attic and redecorated the downstairs with Harmony posters and album covers.

And as an early Christmas present, we've redecorated both your bedrooms in Harmony motif -- wallpaper, curtains, bedspreads. You'll love it!

Sweet harmony and melody to you both.

Mom

P.S. Your camp photos are adorable! I hung them on the refrigerator under our "We ♥ Harmony" magnet. Will you please ask the Harmonys if we can order extra copies when we come for Sibling Appreciation Day?

**Arc de Triomphe du Carrousel
Paris, France**

My rarest little Gems,

Swimming, fishing and canoeing?

It's true. Those activities have a certain, *je ne sais quoi*, rustic charm about them. But let's remember who we are, dears.

Your yachting coach will be none too pleased to hear you've been sailing canoes. And I dare not tell your polo instructor you've been riding *burros*.

I sent you to that quaint camp in the American Middle West so that you might improve your sibling skills. But perhaps two weeks of this working class world is quite enough. Or am I overreacting? Say the word and I shall come retrieve you.

Awaiting your response with love,
I am,

Your Mum

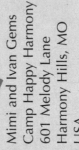

POSTES 3.20
RÉPUBLIQUE FRANÇAISE

PARIS
16
juillet
FRANCE

**PAR AVION
AIR MAIL**

INCOMING MAIL

Forward to Lyle for Incineration

Mimi and Ivan Gems
Camp Happy Harmony
601 Melody Lane
Harmony Hills, MO
USA

THINGS TO DO THIS WEEK:

☐ Work on bus design. Send second payment to Beautiful Buses.

☐ Sign loan papers at bank. Tell loan officers we'll be able to pay off loan when we sell camp. Turn on that Harmony va va va voom magic.
(Wear red silk pant suit.)

☐ Tell real estate agent no "For Sale" signs to be posted on property until L is gone.

☐ Have Dolly record national anthem for my tape.

THEIR BUNKS

my hot tub + dressing room →

my bedroom →

my tv room →

DOROTHY

CAMP HAPPY HARMONY LEDGER

Week of July 16 - 22

DATE	DESCRIPTION	✓	+ INCOME	− EXPENSES
7/17	Royalties		19.86	
7/17	Pawn Daryl's watch		32.99	
7/18	Performance at Dagwood Dog Races		75.00	
7/17	Loan from 1st Ozark Country Meadow Bank		30,000.00	
			30,127.85	
7/16	Director's salary			2,000.00
7/22	Other staff salary			1,000.00
7/17	Second payment on tour bus			12,000.00
7/18	Groceries (for us)			512.36
7/21	Groceries (for kids)			7.89
7/22	Ozark Mtn. Electric Company			379.52
	DISCONNECT A/C IN BROTHERS' BUNKS!			
7/22	Miscellaneous expenses			725.50
				16,625.26

Weekly Balance: $13,502.59

Last Week's Balance: -$13,081.71

Current Balance: $420.88

PAWN PALACE
faux designer watch
$32.99

SAVE-MORE
WHOLESALE FOODS
Damaged and Dented
But Still Pretty OK Groceries
bread (week old) $4.36
radishes $3.52
COST: $7.88

BEAUT
The Ozarks' House
Client Name:
Dorothy Harmony
tummy toner treatment
bottom booster bath
eyelash extensions
Fee: $725.50

Gourmet Goodies
Fabulous Food for Fabulous People
caviar
oysters
mussels
jumbo shrimp (30 lbs.)
marmalade
croissants
imported cocoa
lamb chops
mint jelly
pecans
artichokes
diet pills (fudge flavor)
TOTAL: $512.36
DELIVER TO CAMP HAPPY HARMONY
(back entrance) — C/O DOROTHY

WEEK THREE CLASS SCHEDULE

SISTERS	BROTHERS
Monday	
Want Not, Waist Not	Strong and Silent
The Harmony Gals' Diet Tips	The Brothers' Guide to Success
Instructor: Darlene	Instructor: Dale
Place: Wisteria Cafeteria	Place: Melody Mansion
Tuesday	
Dollars and Sense	Goat Milk: It's Not Just for
Budgeting Your Allowance	Breakfast Anymore!
Instructor: Dorothy	Instructor: Dwayne
Place: Melody Mansion	Place: Wisteria Cafeteria
Wednesday	
Lend Me Your Ears!	Ready, Aim, Bulls-Eye!
Accessorize with Earrings	Bow and Arrow class
Instructor: Darlene	Instructor: Daryl
Place: Wardrobe Abode	Place: Target range
Letters home due today	
Thursday	
Watch Me Dance!	Shining Shoes Is Fun!
Instructor: Dolly	Instructor: Dwayne
Place: Melody Mansion	Place: Dwayne's closet
Friday	
Ironing Contest (Formerly:	Movin' and Groovin'
How Many of Darlene's Dresses	Dance Steps 2 Die 4
Can You Iron In An Hour?)	Instructor: Dwayne
Instructor: Darlene	Place: Melody Mansion
Place: Wardrobe Abode	
Saturday	
Scour with Power!	Synchronized Lawn Mowing
The Art of Bathroom Cleaning	Grab a Mower and Let's Go!
structor: Darlene	Instructor: Dale
e: Melody Mansion	Place: Meet at equipment shed
Sunday	
d Relaxation	Rest and Relaxation
ve Inspection	White Glove Inspection
	Letters home due today

ACTIVITIES WEEK THREE

GIRLS	BOYS
continue painting theater in Melody Mansion	strip + refinish all woodwork
feed pigs/ goats/burros (every morning)	gather eggs; milk goats (every morning)
remove all dande-lions from property	retile bath-rooms (all)
trim hooves on goats/burros	wash dishes (all meals)
sew and hang curtains for all windows	build stone wall (2 miles)
dig hole for reflecting pond in front of Melody Mansion	plant 75 cherry trees (Melody Mansion lawn)
write one letter home	write one letter home

Weather Forecast:

Hotter than a Harmony No. 1 hit! Drought advisory posted for all counties in southern Missouri. No-burn order in effect for entire Ozark region. No fires!

THIS WEEK AT THE WISTERIA CAFETERIA:

	MON	TUES	WED	THUR	FRI	SAT & SUN
	toast	toast	cereal	toast	cereal	toast + cereal!
	pb & j sandwich	cheese sandwich	pb & j sandwich	cheese sandwich	pb & j sandwich	pb & j & cheese sandwich!

Each camper will be served a meal specially prepared by Chef Dolly herself!
Bon appetit!!

CAMP·O·GRAM

Dear Charlotte, Mimi and Barbie Q.:

You'll never imagine what we discovered
this morning in the Melody Mansion when we
were refinishing the woodwork. There we
were, the three of us, labouring like
worker bees, whereupon the sun shone in
through the window like a spotlight, and —

*Hot tamale, Ivan! Let me tell 'em. We
found Mimi's box of chocolates.
Right there on Dorothy's desk.*

WE STOLE IT. BUT IT'S NOT REALLY STEALING IF
WE RETURN THE CHOCOLATES TO THEIR RIGHTFUL
OWNER, IS IT?

*Course not! Lyle says cowboy code
demands we steal 'em back for Miss
Mimi.*

I quite agree. Until we see you all
tonight at the outlaw chow,

We are,

Your crusaders in chocolate,

Ivan   *Brisket*   CHARLIE

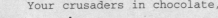

 # CAMP-O-GRAM

Dearest Ivan, Brisket and Charlie:

Many thanks for returning the chocolates to me. Do let's save them for dessert tonight. Divided seven ways won't leave much for anyone, especially since Dorothy apparently helped herself to more than half the box.

But heck, even a little chocolate beats those Crabby Carob Bars they tried to serve us last night at supper. That crud smelled worse than the breath of a dozen dead armadillos.

Speaking of crabby, you guys wouldn't believe the screaming match we heard this morning between those songbirds of harmony. Dolly, Darlene and Dorothy were really going at it. And they say they'd rather sing than fight 'cause being polite is such a delight?

HA! If they're polite, I'm Snow White.

— Barbie Q.

Mimi

Charlotte

78

But if you think the Harmony sisters' squabbles are bad, you ought to see their brothers.

DEAR CHARLOTTE,
BARBIE Q. AND MIMI:

HA! IS RIGHT. MORE LIKE THESE HARMONYS WOULD RATHER FIGHT THAN WORK, 'CAUSE THEY'RE ALL A BUNCH OF JERKS.

mail. This morning after quite a dramatic exchange with Dale and Daryl. It appeared the good doctor received some bad news in the mail. He seemed to be venting his frustration by poking his younger brothers in the eyes with a mature zucchini squash. Quite the gentleman, that Dwayne.

Enough already about those lousy Harmonys. See y'all tonight in the orchard for supper.

Bring your appetites and them chocolates; I'm fixin' catfish chowder à la Brisket and goat cheese chocolate cheesecake à la Mimi.

Brisket Ivan

CHARLIE

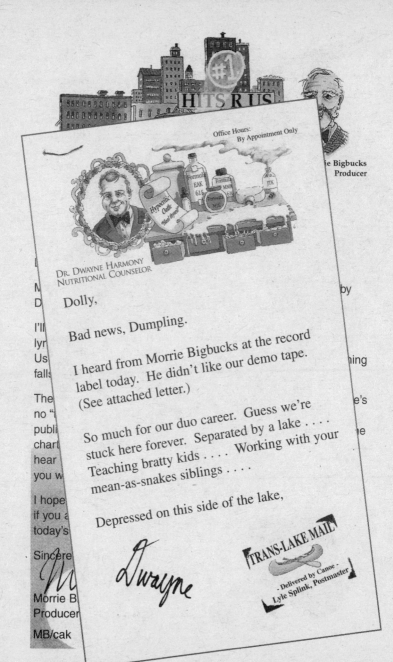

DR. DWAYNE HARMONY
NUTRITIONAL COUNSELOR

Office Hours:
By Appointment Only

Dolly,

Bad news, Dumpling.

I heard from Morrie Bigbucks at the record
label today. He didn't like our demo tape.
(See attached letter.)

So much for our duo career. Guess we're
stuck here forever. Separated by a lake . . . .
Teaching bratty kids . . . . Working with your
mean-as-snakes siblings . . . .

Depressed on this side of the lake,

Dwayne

TRANS-LAKE MAIL
- Delivered by Canoe -
Lyle Splink, Postmaster

Music Row
Nashville, TN

Morrie Bigbucks
Producer

July 14

Dwayne Harmony
Camp Happy Harmony
601 Melody Lane
Harmony Hills, Missouri

Dwayne,

Many thanks for sending me a copy of your demo tape, "Duets by Dwayne and Dolly: Just the Two of Us!"

I'll cut right to the chase, Dwayne. The tape is no good. The lyrics are corny (especially the song "Oh, How You've Missed Us!") and the vocals, especially yours, are weak. The whole thing falls flat.

The problem is simple: There's no tension in your songs. There's no "there" there, as we say in the music biz. The music-buying public has changed since the old days when your family ruled the charts. Kids today want rawness, rage, energy. They want to hear the bitter tragedy of human existence — the bite of life, if you will — set to music.

I hope you're not discouraged. I'd love to hear more of your work if you and your sister can find a way to make it more palatable to today's sophisticated listeners.

Sincerely,

Morrie Bigbucks

Morrie Bigbucks
Producer

MB/cak

WISTERIA CAFETERIA
COOKIN' WITH DOLLY

Dwayney sweetie,

We can't give up that easily, darling. You know as well as I do that we were born to sing as a duo. We're the only ones around here (not counting Lyle) who can even carry a tune. If only we could perform together, just the two of us. Even if it's for small crowds, we could show people what we're capable of. Word would get out how powerful our music is.

I'm going to ask Dorothy about the possibility of you and me singing a duet at Sibling Appreciation Day. Not much chance of her agreeing to it, but it's worth a shot.

Never give up, angel! I haven't. Nor should you.

Your
Dolly

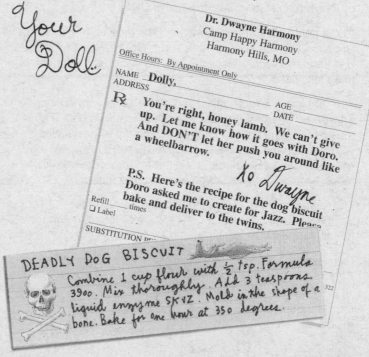

Dr. Dwayne Harmony
Camp Happy Harmony
Harmony Hills, MO

Office Hours: By Appointment Only

NAME **Dolly,**
ADDRESS

Rx
AGE
DATE

You're right, honey lamb. We can't give up. Let me know how it goes with Doro. And DON'T let her push you around like a wheelbarrow.

Xo Dwayne

P.S. Here's the recipe for the dog biscuit Doro asked me to create for Jazz. Please bake and deliver to the twins.

Refill ____ times
❏ Label

SUBSTITUTION P

DEADLY DOG BISCUIT

Combine 1 cup flour with ½ tsp. Formula 3900. Mix thoroughly. Add 3 teaspoons liquid enzyme SKVZ. Mold in the shape of a bone. Bake for one hour at 350 degrees.

Dwayne,

Why do I even try? Here's a play-by-play of my request and Dorothy's response:

ME: Doro, do you think maybe Dwayne and I could sing a duet at Sibling Appreciation Day?

DORO: No.

ME: Not even just a verse or two?

DORO: No.

ME: And why not?

DORO: Because I'm singing two solos. That's why.

ME: YOU'RE singing two solos? That's a big laugh.

DORO: And what's so funny about that, Dogface?

ME: Just the fact that you can't carry a tune in a bucket.

DORO: And your point is?

ME: Oh, I don't know. Just the fact that YOU'RE not actually going to sing. You're just going to lip-synch MY vocals, aren't you, Doro? Just mouth the words wike a wittle puppet, wight?

DORO: In fact, I am, Dogface. Have you got a problem with that?

ME: Yes, I do, Doro. I mean, come on. You and your tricks are what got us in this mess in the first place.

DORO: My tricks? What about you and your trick, Doctor Wayne?

ME: His name is now Dwayne. And what about us, any-
          way?

DORO: Oh, right. As if you don't know. Falling in
          love with the slimeball we hired to be our
          brother. That's reeeeeal smooth, Dolly.

ME: Well, at least I'm honest about my feelings.
          And at least I can sing. More than I can say
          about some people around here.

DORO: Oh, yeah?

ME: Yeah.

DORO: Yeah? Well at least I don't wear those goofy
          dresses like Duh-rlene.

ME: Yeah, me neither. What a dingbat she is.

DORO: You got that right, Dogface. Hey, is there any
          of that pudding left over from last night?

ME: Just the medicated stuff for the brats.

DORO: Forget it. Make me a hot fudge sundae on the
          q.t. and bring it to my office.

TRANS-LAKE MAIL
- Delivered by Canoe -
Lyle Splink, Postmaster

DR. DWAYNE HARMONY
NUTRITIONAL COUNSELOR

Office Hours:
By Appointment Only

Dolly,

Now your sister is calling ME a slimeball? That's it. I've had it with your family.

Bigbucks wants tension? The music-buying public wants tragedy? How about this:

Four members of the Harmony family (Dorothy, Darlene, Daryl and Dale) die suddenly from a mysterious, incurable, untraceable disease. (I'll take care of that part. I didn't get a degree in nutrition for nothing!)

The remaining two Harmonys (you and me) are shocked, grief-stricken and saddened beyond words. Our only solace is our music, which we reluctantly share with the music-buying public as a way of healing the loss of our beloved siblings.

Not bad, eh? And just think: When we ditch the others, you and I can finally sing the songs we've always loved and live the life we've always planned.

Dollface, I can't stand living under the thumb of Doro and the others any longer. And I can't bear to be separated from you by this fish-clogged lake. Without your blankety-blank brothers and sisters around, we could finally come clean about our relationship and get married.

I could go into town later today and call Bigbucks with the bad news about the deadly disease eating away at our brothers and sisters. What do you think?

Slimelessly yours,

Dwayne

TRANS-LAKE MAIL

- Delivered by Canoe -
Lyle Splink, Postmaster

85

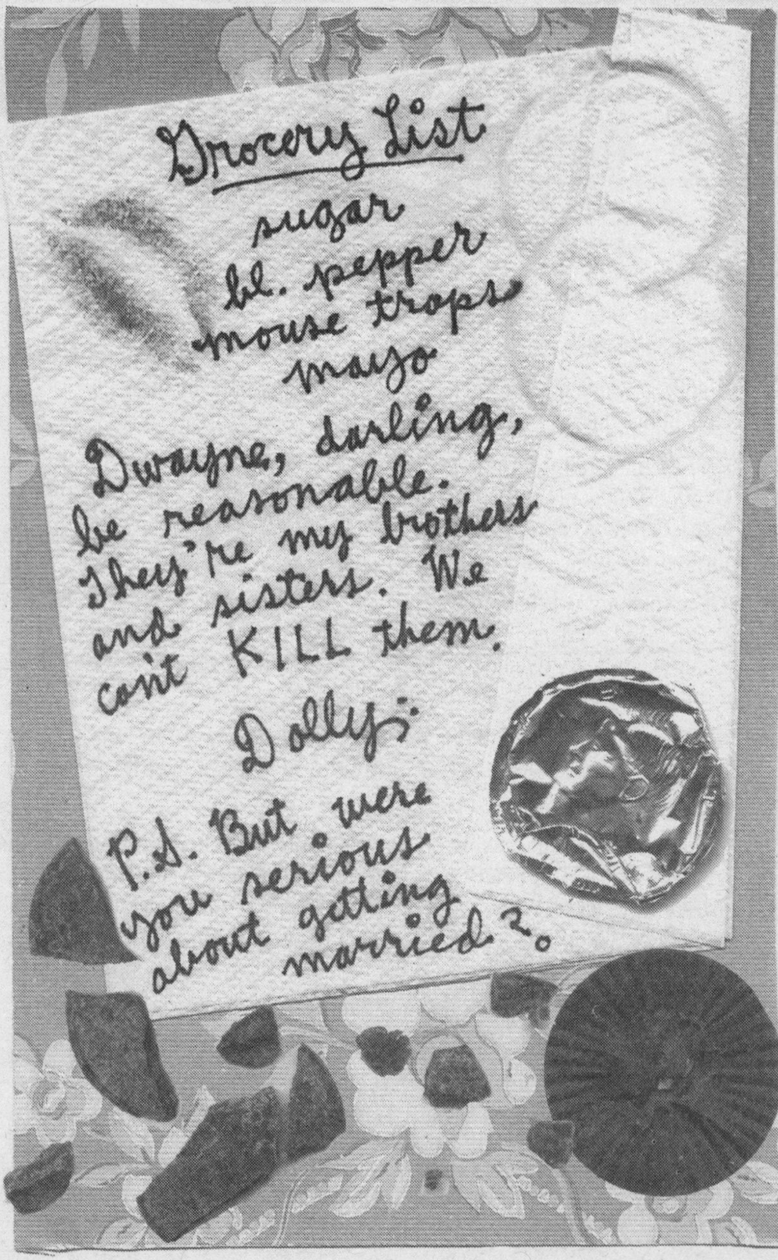
Grocery List
sugar
bl. pepper
mouse traps
mayo
Dwayne, darling,
be reasonable.
They're my brothers
and sisters. We
can't KILL them.
Dolly
P.S. But were
you serious
about getting
married?

DR. DWAYNE HARMONY
NUTRITIONAL COUNSELOR

Dollface,

Let me get this straight: You're cool about offing Lyle, the only decent one (besides you) in the whole act. But you think the others should be spared?

Get real. Those saber-toothed sisters of yours have never done anything but ruin your career. Dorothy steals the show with YOUR voice, while Darlene tries to upstage you both in her eye-popping (and button-popping) costumes.

You should hear the way Dale and Daryl talk about you behind your back. "Two-ton Dolly, heavy as a trolley," and all that. And every time you get mad and waddle off in a huff, the twins laugh and say that your fat jiggles in your stockings like custard in cheesecloth. (But I *like* that about you, Dumpling!)

Of course I'm serious about getting married. But it's your choice—them or me. Choose or lose, baby.

Dwayne

Dale and Daryl are making fun of my weight again?! That does it. I choose you to be my partner in song and life. Call Bigbucks and let's start cookin'.
Dolly

P.S. You know I can't help my weight. It's my thyroid.

A Note from the Harmony Gals
Sweet Sister Sings . . .

TO: Charlotte **FR:** *Dorothy*
Mimi *Darlene*
Barbie Q. *Dolley*

Top o' the morning, sisters!

Letters home are due today. This will be your last one, since no letters are required during the final week of camp, Wilderness Adventure Week.

Smiles!

From the Horse's Mouth

BARBIE Q. ROAST

Wednesday

Chuck Roast
Chuck Wagon Ranch
Porterhouse, Texas

UNOPENED

Some Daddy you are.

Oh, yeah. You pretend you love Brisket and me. Then you turn around and send us to this creepy-as-cat's-guts camp! Lucky for me I've made some good amigos here. Even Brisket's being kind of a sweet thing for a change.

Not that you care. I reckon you're not even fixin' to round us up at the end of the month. You'll probably just leave us here forever — or until Brisket and me bite the dust and become a pair of bleached and dried carcasses. Is that what you want? IS IT?

Well then, Big Daddy, I guess it's time to wake up and smell the bacon bits. What am I saying? Just this: Goodbye, Big Daddy. Goodbye and good riddance.

Your only cowgirl (but no more),

OUTGOING MAIL

Forward to Lyle for Incineration

— Barbie Q.

P.S. And don't even think about riding my horses.

MIMI GEMS

[UNOPENED]

18 July

Dear Mummy,

I've been gone only three weeks, but it seems much longer. Especially since I haven't heard from you. Are you well? I do hope so.

So much has happened since I last saw you. I don't wish to worry you, but the Harmony sisters are not what they seem. I know they looked sweet as candied violets in the brochure, but they're utterly cruel and hateful to us and to each other.

I overheard Dolly and Dorothy yelling at one another again this morning. It was positively unnerving, like nails on a chalkboard -- or white shoes in autumn! I had no idea how frightful that kind of bickering sounds. You'll be pleased to know I've made a solemn vow never to raise my voice at Ivan again.

Speaking of whom, your son has been almost a gentleman here at camp. He's socializing with the other children and he even complimented me on the mural I'm painting in the Melody Mansion. I must admit the project is coming along quite nicely. I'll sketch a small likeness of the mural so you can judge for yourself.

Anyway, Mumsly dear, I hope to see you on Sibling Appreciation Day. That is, provided I survive this highly unusual Harmony experience. But if not, I know my remaining days on this earth will be most exciting. Hope you're enjoying Paris.

Kisses to you,

Mimi

90

Rural Route 1, Box 257
Stopsign, Illinois

7/18
OUTGOING MAIL
Forward to Lyle for Incineration

Dear Mom and Dad,

Charlie says he's written to you and asked you to come pick us up. I think he even tried to call. Still — nothing. No letters. No phone calls. No you. At least I have Charlie (who, believe it or not, has been half-way OK lately) and the new friends I've made here at camp.

Brisket has been cooking for all of us. Last night his sister made Mimi and me some really funky overalls out of these dorky dresses Darlene Harmony gave us to wear. I've been teaching everyone the dances the kids do back home. I'm even making up new steps to go with some of Charlie's songs. Did you know he can write songs? I didn't. Our friend Lyle says Charlie's a natural songwriter.

Lyle's the only normal grownup here. The Harmonys are complete nutcases and not at all what you said they'd be like. When you return for Charlie and me, we'll introduce you to the REAL Harmonys and to all the friends we've made here.

Until then, I'm still confused about your reasons for sending us to this weird camp.

Love anyhow,

Charlotte

DOROTHY APPROVED

Dear (insert parental reference here),

This is turning out ~~~~~ ummer of my life! I'm so glad you didn't sen~~~~~ Happy Harmony is the o~~~~~ d every summer!

And right here i~~~~~ ek from Sunday. That's t~~~~~ also Sibling Appreci~~~~~ eat!

Since our arri~~~~~ er's name here) and I h~~~~~ theme song, "We'd Rather~~~~~ h A Delight." Just wait till yo~~~~~

You'll probably want to bring your ca~~~~~ can get a picture of us wearing our Kooky Kamp Klothes, designed by the very talented (and sweet as sugar!) Darlene Harmony. Bring some extra money, too, so we can buy some Kooky Kamp Klothes to take home.

I just can't get enough of these Harmonys!

(insert daughter's name here)

Dorothy,

Here are the photos and form letters to send parents.

Darlene

P.S. Why is Lyle still here? If he's not gone soon, I'm moving my stuff into your chalet and your stuff into the Wardrobe Abode. Then you can see how you like living in this little rat hole.

See ya soon!

A MEMO FROM
DOROTHY HARMONY

TO: DARLENE

FR: DOROTHY

RE: WHY ARE YOU SO DUMB?

STAFF NOTE

Do you think I LIKE having L around here?

Do you think I LIKE having the loan officers from the bank call me 50 times a day, asking when I'm going to pay back the money I borrowed to cover our expenses on this dump?

Do you think this is the LIFE I envisioned for myself — singing the National Anthem at dog races and discount grocery store openings?

DUH-rlene! We ALL want Lyle out of the way so we can finally sell this overgrown weedpatch and launch our comeback tour.

I'm marching over to talk to the twins right now.

Dorothy

PRIVATE

CAMP·O·GRAM

Brisket, Charlie and Ivan:

Have y'all heard the news? Lyle took Jazz to the animal hospital this morning. Lyle thinks he was poisoned!

Poor Lyle is panicked. He doesn't know what caused it. Says it's a mystery. Ivan, we told him he should talk to you since you're the mystery expert around here.

It's such a horror, isn't it? Lyle has been so kind to us these past three weeks, delivering our Camp-O-Grams and giving us rides in his canoe at all hours of the day and night. We're painting him a portrait for his cabin. Perhaps you boys could think of some way to cheer Lyle up, too.

Brisket, could you maybe fix an extra-special supper tonight in Lyle's honor? All your cooking tastes good as grits, but you catch my meaning.

And Charlie, maybe you could write a song about Jazz. I know Lyle would treasure it.

Charlotte

Mimi

- Barbie Q.

TRANS·LAKE MAIL
- Delivered by Canoe -
Lyle Splink, Postmaster

94

CAMP-O-GRAM

Barbie Q., Charlotte and Mimi:

It appears bad news travels quickly.
Lyle told us about Jazz when he
stopped by to deliver your letter.

*I never saw such a sad cowpuncher in
all my born days. Besides us, that old
dog is Lyle's only friend around here.*

LET'S MAKE TONIGHT OPERATION: CHEER UP
LYLE. WITH PLENTY OF GOOD FOOD, MUSIC,
DANCING AND FRIENDS, WE'LL HELP LYLE FORGET
HIS SADNESS — FOR AT LEAST A COUPLE OF
HOURS.

Until we see you in the orchard tonight
at 9:30,

Ivan   CHARLIE   Brisket

"A TRIBUTE TO JAZZ"

BY CHARLIE LEE

95

DATE **Wednesday** HOUR **5 p.m.**

TO **Dale and Daryl**

WHILE YOU WERE OUT

M **YOUR SISTER (AND BOSS!)**

OF _____

PHONE _____

☐ Telephoned ☐ Returned Call ☐ Left Package
☐ Please Call ☒ Was In ☒ Please See Me
☐ Will Call Again ☐ Won't Call ☒ Important!

MESSAGE: *I am writing these words very slowly because I know how difficult reading is for you clowns. In fact, I'll make it real simple: The dog is gone. So what's the hold up NOW?*

SIGNED **Dorothy**

96

DA TWINS

DUH-orothy!

We know the dog is gone.
We're the ones who shoved the
poison doggie biscuit down its
throat at 3 o'clock this morning and
watched the little mutt keel over.

The problem now is the kids. We
planned to drown Lyle yesterday, but
there were too many ~~minachur~~ little
witnesses running around.
There's always at least one
punk down at the dock,
giving him
a letter to deliver or just
hanging around.

Maybe we should off the kids, too.
Just to be safe. We're rethinking
our ~~stratidgee~~ plan. What do you
say, Doro?

D and D

TRANS-LAKE MAIL
· Delivered by Canoe ·
Lyle Splink, Postmaster

97

STAFF NOTE

Dale and Daryl,

Thinking? You two idiots? Oh, please. Save the baloney for lunch. Of course we can't kill the brats. Their parents will be here a week from Sunday to pick them up.

I'll have Dolly increase the levels of medication in the kids' food. But if the snot-nosed monkeys are still the only thing preventing you from dealing with *the L situation*, wait until Wilderness Adventure Week (Monday through Friday of next week). The kids will be camping in the woods. Do the deed then.

Also, you hay-bales-for-brains might want to practice a little discretion in your TRANS-LAKE correspondence. Remember who delivers the mail around here.

'Nuff said. Keep me posted on your plans. And quit calling me Doro.

Dorothy

P.S. Besides, I hear the mutt isn't even dead -- just sick. Can't you bozos do anything right?

Dorothy,

Look, sis. We're going to kill Lyle, just like you told us to. (Woops! So much for ~~discreshun~~ that other stuff.)

Later, Doro.

Dand D

Camp Happy Harmony

601 Melody Lane
Harmony Hills, MO

Charlotte,
Use your flashlight to read this letter.
I typed it with my invisible ink ribbon.

TRANS-LAKE MAIL

Lyl...

Well, that was quite a gala last night. Wasn't it positively ducky to see Lyle smiling again? Chop chop!

And who knew Lyle could play the guitar? He's going to give Charlie lessons and teach him how to write songs like the professionals do. Seems Lyle knew all the famous songwriters back in the old days. He told me he even wrote a few songs when he was on the road with the Harmonys. I asked him to play one but he declined, saying they were "no good." I'm not certain if he was talking about the songs or the Harmonys.

Speaking of which, what were you girls talking -- or rather, whispering -- about last night? A secret, perhaps? Do tell, won't you?

Dear Ivan,

It was more of a mystery than a secret, but I'll tell you anyway.

Remember when I was teaching you all the new dance I made up? I was using my flashlight so everyone could see my feet and follow the steps?

Well, every time we did the three-step turn, my flashlight lit up the big apple tree in the middle of the orchard, and I saw something I hadn't noticed before -- a heart carved in the trunk of the tree and these words: "Dolly Harmony + Wayne Dumbuddy = ♥ 4ever."

Dumbuddy must've been Dolly's old boyfriend. That's what we were howling about. We asked Lyle for details about Dolly's love life, but he just shook his head and mumbled, "Those two . . . Those two . . . ."

Whoever he was, he and Dolly must've been quite the gruesome twosome if that's all Lyle would say about them.

I've got to wrap this up. Dolly's walking in the door right this sec—

Charlotte

P.S. Ivan, please tell Brisket that last night's dinner was peachy!
Mimi

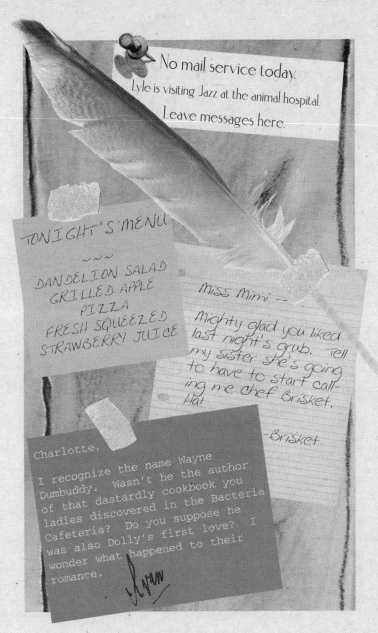

No mail service today.
Lyle is visiting Jazz at the animal hospital.
Leave messages here.

TONIGHT'S MENU

~~~

DANDELION SALAD
GRILLED APPLE
PIZZA
FRESH SQUEEZED
STRAWBERRY JUICE

Miss Mimi --

Mighty glad you liked last night's grub. Tell my sister she's going to have to start calling me chef Brisket. Ha!

-Brisket

Charlotte,

I recognize the name Wayne Dumbuddy. Wasn't he the author of that dastardly cookbook you ladies discovered in the Bacteria Cafeteria? Do you suppose he was also Dolly's first love? I wonder what happened to their romance.

Ryan

Music Row
Nashville, TN

Good golly, Miss Dolly! Take a look at this letter! Now to concoct a prescription for Ozark Mountain Cabin Fever.

XXoo! Dwayne

July 16

Dwayne Harmony
Camp Happy Harmony
601 Melody Lane
Harmony Hills, Missouri

Dear Dwayne,

Please accept the sincere condolences of everyone here at #1 Hits R Us. To lose one sibling is bad enough. But for four of your brothers and sisters to be stricken with the deadly Ozark Mountain Cabin Fever is . . . Well, it's simply beyond words.

I'm not familiar with this particular disease, but I can understand why you didn't want to go into details on the phone. Suffice it to say we're thinking of you all during this difficult time.

I'm sure your duo career with Dolly is the last thing on your mind. But when you feel up to it, I hope you'll give me a call so we can discuss your plans for the future.

I'll cut right to the chase, Dwayne. Your voice can't help but resonate with the pain and raw emotion you're feeling. If you're interested, if you're even able, we'd like to release your and Dolly's first duo album. Enclosed please find a contract.

Our publicity department believes the moving story of how you and your sister cope with the devastating death of your siblings (and best friends!) will make you and Dolly shoo-ins on the talk show circuit. Also, as you know, our parent company, STARS R US, owns a major motion picture studio and publishing house. I'm confident the producers and editors will be very interested in a movie and book deal based on your dramatic story.

Again, please know how very sorry I am to hear of your family's tragedy.

Sincerely,

Morrie Bigbucks

Morrie Bigbucks
Producer

MB/cak

(Enclosed: Contr

CONTRACT

#1 Hits R Us
and
Dolly and Dwayne Harmony

This agreement, made July 16, between Dolly and Dwayne Harmony and #1 Hits R Us, for the purpose of creating musical properties (tapes, compact discs, etc.) and associated products (films, TV shows, t-shirts, posters, bumper stickers, lunch boxes, etc.), provides that Dolly and Dwayne Harmony shall receive:

ONE MILLION DOLLARS ($1,000,000) upon release of their first album for #1 Hits R Us, and thereafter, TEN PERCENT OF PROFITS.

Dolly Harmony

Dwayne Harmony

Morrie Bigbucks

Morrie Bigbucks
Producer

WISTERIA CAFETERIA

COOKIN' WITH DOLLY

TRANS-LAKE MAIL
- Delivered by Canoe -
Lyle Splink, Postmaster

Oh my gosh, Dwayne!

It's FINALLY going to happen for us. A duo career!
But first, you've got some damage control to do.

Get into town later today and call Bigbucks. We need
to make sure he realizes how important it is that news
of this "tragedy" isn't leaked to the press. The last
thing we want around here is a bunch of reporters
asking Dorothy, Darlene and the twins how it feels to
be dying from Ozark Mountain Cabin Fever. (Where
do you come up with this stuff, anyway?)

Hurry, darling. You know how fast those buzzards in
the press are.

Your Doll

K-NEWZ TV

LIVE AT FIVE
with
Harry and Bunny

TRANSCRIPT
July 19

BUNNY: Good evening and welcome to Live at Five. Tonight's top story is going to come as a shock to a lot of viewers who grew up listening to the sweet sounds of harmony. We're talking, of course, about The Harmony Family Singers, those melodious siblings who, by their love and devotion to one another, set an example for families everywhere. Though still unconfirmed, we have a report that four of The Harmony Family Singers — Dorothy, Darlene, Dale and Daryl — have been diagnosed with a fatal disease known only as Ozark Mountain Cabin Fever. K-NEWZ reporter Harry is on the scene in Harmony Hills, Missouri. Harry, what can you tell us about this breaking news?

HARRY: Well, Bunny, we don't know much more than what you've just reported. The news is still sketchy, but industry insiders say it's true. Only Dolly and Dwayne seem to have escaped the curse of this rare and deadly disease. From what we're told, Bunny, the other four Harmonys have just a short time to live. Hard to believe, isn't it? I don't know about you, but the Harmony kids have always seemed like my own brothers and sisters. Their weekly TV show was a staple of my childhood. I never missed it.

BUNNY: I know what you mean, Harry. "We'd Rather Sing Than Fight, 'Cause Being Polite Is Such A Delight" is still my favorite song. I can assure you and all of our viewers that we'll be following this story very closely. And now on to other news of the day . . . .

OFFICE OF
THE
DIRECTOR

MELODY
MANSION

A MEMO FROM
DOROTHY HARMONY

TO:	DWAYNE, DARYL, DALE, DOLLY, DARLENE and LYLE
FR:	DOROTHY
RE:	BIG NEWS!

Good news, gang. The senior editor from *The Main Street Journal* just called. He wants to do a story on The Harmony Family Singers and, as he put it, the "dramatic new developments" in our lives.

This will be big exposure for us. Looks like my marketing efforts are finally paying off! (Lucky ONE of us around here is doing her job.)

They're sending a reporter and I want to be ready. We need to get our house in order. I'm talking inside (dusting, vacuuming) and outside (grass, hedges). Per usual, we'll have the kids do the bulk of the work. We might want to hold a couple of them back from the Wilderness Adventure nonsense so they can wax floors, etc.

Our main task will be to get rid of all the junk around here we don't need. I'm thinking in particular of some excess baggage we must dispose of. (Listening, Dale and Daryl?)

Details to follow as I hear them.

Dorothy

STAFF NOTE

Dorothy (or should I say Miss Bossypants?):

YOU'RE the one who made that stupid deal with Lyle in the first place, so getting rid of him is YOUR responsibility.

Darlene

A Note from the Harmony Gals
Sweet Sisters Sing . . .

TO: Charlotte **FR:** *Dorothy Darlene*
Mimi *Dolley*
Barbie Q.

Company's coming! We want to look our very best when your parents come for Sibling Appreciation Day a week from Sunday.

That's why we'll conduct a White Glove Inspection this Sunday night. You must receive a passing score on the inspection in order to participate in the Wilderness Adventure campout next week.

So let's mop till we drop and dust till we bust!

A HARMONIC NOTE FROM YOUR BROTHERS

TO:
Ivan **FR:** *Dwayne*
Charlie *Dale Daryl*
Brisket

Howdy, fellas!

We've got some uptown company coming for Sibling Appreciation Day and we want to look our downtown best. So what do you say we double up on the chores around here? Who's game for some fast tempo vacuuming and dusting? Hit it, boys!

We'll grade your cleaning efforts on Sunday night during White Glove Inspection. If you don't pass, you can't go on the Wilderness Adventure campout.

Letters home are due Sunday, before White Glove Inspection.

From the Plate of
BRISKET ROAST

Sunday

Chuck Roast
Chuck Wagon Ranch
Porterhouse, Texas

Well, Big Daddy,

I don't know what you'll be more riled by — the fact that my life is in mighty serious peril* here at camp, OR the fact that I've become a vegetarian. Take your pick.

Or maybe neither one bothers you. Maybe you don't give a roach's rear about me and Barbie Q. That's how it seems anyway. You don't write or call or send me the stuff I ask for.

I DON'T CARE! Barbie Q. and me both have made us some dang good friends up here, and we're all watching out for one another. We're having a meeting (the six of us) later tonight to plan our strategy for Wilderness Adventure Week. But you probably don't care about that either.

Your only son,

Brisket Roast
(in case you've forgotten my name)

*This here's a five-dollar word I learned from an English feller. It means something like getting stuck in quicksand with a passel of starvin' rattlers.

POST CARD

OUTGOING MAIL

Forward to Lyle for Incineration

Mr. and Mrs. Lee

Rural Route 1, Box 257

Stopsign, Illinois

CAMP HAPPY HARMONY   HARMONY HILLS, MISSOURI

HARMONY
USA
32

July 22

Mom and Dad:

I wish I knew you were as concerned about Charlotte's and my safety here at camp as I am. However, I must assume from your silence that you neither miss nor care about your only children.

Disappointed,

Charlie

109

Ivan Gems

22 July

Dearest Mum,

As they say in dimestore novels, the plot
thickens. Unfortunately, some of the clues
(e.g. the tainted food) have been a bit
unsavoury. The scene grew even darker this
week when a healthy dog was discovered poisoned. No clues. No suspects. No motive
that we know of. Very curious, wouldn't you
agree?

To crack the case, I suggested we work in
pairs during Wilderness Adventure Week.
Mimi and I will intentionally fail tonight's
White Glove Inspection so we can stay close
to camp and do a little on-site research.
Brisket and Barbie Q. will pass the test so
they can explore the woods and see what
other clues they can uncover. Charlotte and
Charlie must also pass inspection so they
can work as needed, either indoors or out,
depending on what we find.

We'll keep each other informed via Camp-
O-Grams, with Lyle serving as command cen-
tral. He says he's never seen a bunch of
"young'uns" have so much fun.

I wish you were here, Mum, so I could
tell you these latest travails in person.
Neither Mimi nor I have heard from you since
we left England. Do my letters bore you?
I pray not. You know I want nothing more
than to be a mystery writer when I grow up.
And to think I may have stumbled across my
first *whodunit* here at camp!

White Glove Inspection begins in five
minutes. I must away.

Ivan

110

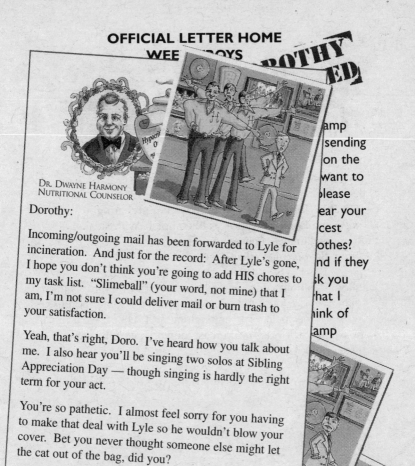

OFFICIAL LETTER HOME
WEE[ ]BOYS

DR. DWAYNE HARMONY
NUTRITIONAL COUNSELOR

Dorothy:

Incoming/outgoing mail has been forwarded to Lyle for incineration. And just for the record: After Lyle's gone, I hope you don't think you're going to add HIS chores to my task list. "Slimeball" (your word, not mine) that I am, I'm not sure I could deliver mail or burn trash to your satisfaction.

Yeah, that's right, Doro. I've heard how you talk about me. I also hear you'll be singing two solos at Sibling Appreciation Day — though singing is hardly the right term for your act.

You're so pathetic. I almost feel sorry for you having to make that deal with Lyle so he wouldn't blow your cover. Bet you never thought someone else might let the cat out of the bag, did you?

You just better thank your lucky stars I'm in love with your sister. If it weren't for Dolly, I'd have blown the whistle on this Harmony scam long ago.

Dwayne

(insert son's name here)

The Harmonys Rule!

111

No Meal Is Complete Without A Little Red Meat

Hey there, Barbie Q. and Brisket!

Won't be long till I see you now. I'm preparing a walloping welcome home party for y'all, complete with steaks, ribs, burgers, tamales, fajitas, home fries, corn bread, watermelon, gravy-flavored ice cream and . . . .

Shoot, I plumb can't remember the rest of the grub. Just plan on bringing a big-bellied appetite for some mouth-waterin' red meat. For entertainment, I reckon we'll run us some hayrack rides and grease down some pigs so's we can race 'em.

Here are two more boxes of vittles to hold you over till the welcome home party.

Chow for now,

Big Daddy

INCOMING MAIL

Forward to Lyle for Incineration

UNOPENED

Have you kissed a carnivore today?

112

Rural Route 1, Box 257
Stopsign, Illinois

July 21

Dear Charlotte and Charlie,

We can't wait to see you next week when we come to Camp Happy Harmony! Won't it be fun to have our family picture taken with the famous Harmony Family Singers? Let's plan on using the photo as our Christmas card, okay?

Counting the days till we see you together (and happy?) again at Sibling Appreciation Day. We'll be wearing our favorite "Harmony Begins At Home" sweat-shirts. Don't worry. We've got matching Harmony sweatshirts for you both. Hope they fit!

Love,

Mom and Dad

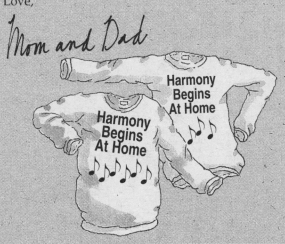

Palais du Luxembourg

My priceless little Gems,

I gather from your last letters that you would rather be at camp in America than with me in Europe. I understand, though it pains me more than you shall ever know.

The unspeakable loneliness of these past few weeks has made me realize that I must learn to accept you both for who you are, rather than for who I want you to be.

Sending you off to camp as I did without your permission was unforgivable. I hope you can find room in your hearts to forgive me, even if you can never forgive one another.

Until I see my precious little Gems next week,

I am, with heartfelt apologies,

Your Mum

Mimi and Ivan Gems
Camp Happy Harmony
601 Melody Lane
Harmony Hills, Missouri
USA

PAR AVION
AIR MAIL

REPUBLIQUE FRANÇAISE
POSTES
3,20
Mont-Saint-Michel

PARIS
24
juillet
FRANCE

INCOMING MAIL

Forward to 125¢ for Unclaimed?

Week of July 23 - 29

THINGS TO DO THIS WEEK:

☐ Put finishing touches on bus design.

☐ Iron things out with Dwayne and Dolly.

☐ Make sure D and D deal with THE L SITUATION this week!

☐ Call funeral home. Ask about discounts for early orders.

☐ Prepare for Sibling Appreciation Day.

My hot tub, sauna, etc.!

my dressing room

my bedroom

my tv video room

, bunks

skylights? Deck?

Dorothy Harmony and...

CAMP HAPPY HARMONY LEDGER

Week of July 23 - 29

DATE	DESCRIPTION	✓	+ INCOME	− EXPENSES
7/24	Royalties		9.13	
7/25	Plasma donation		27.55	
7/25	pawn shop		13.65	
7/25	Loan #2 from 1st Ozark Country Meadow Bank		15,000.00	
			15,050.33	
7/23	Director's salary			2,000.00
7/29	Other staff salary			1,000.00
7/26	Groceries (for us)			573.89
7/27	Groceries (for kids)			0
7/27	Third payment on tour bus			12,000.00
7/29	Miscellaneous expenses			1,025.00
				16,598.89

Weekly Balance: −$1,548.56
Last Week's Balance: $420.88
Current Balance: −$1,127.68

Now we owe $45,000 to 1st Ozark Country Meadow Bank. I HATE bookkeeping!

PAWN PALACE
Dale's bowling trophy
$13.65

BEAU
"CARS TL
Gourmet Goodies
Fabulous Food for Fabulous People
pork chops
imported cheeses
German chocolate cake
salmon spread
marshmallow ice cream
lemon meringue pies (one case)
assorted breads/muffins
ginger ale
chicken wings
TOTAL: $573.89
DELIVER TO CAMP HAPPY HARMONY
(back _____) — C/O DOROTHY
PAYM

SAVE-N
WHOLESAL
Damaged and
But Still Pretty OK
NO ORDER THIS WEEK
COST: $0

BEAUTY HUT
The Ozarks' House of Beauty
Client Name:
Dorothy Harmony
Face-firming therapy
Wrinkle recovery
Fat blaster treatment
Violet-tinted contact lenses
Fee: $1,025

WEEK FOUR
CLASS SCHEDULE
Wilderness Adventure Week

For those of you who passed White Glove Inspection:

You're on your own in the woods for five days!

Use this time to think about the important sibling skills you've learned at Camp Happy Harmony. Reflect on how you can be better brothers and sisters when you return home.

On Sunday, every camper will have an opportunity during the Sibling Appreciation Day program to share (on stage!) the valuable lessons learned at Camp Happy Harmony. Each camper should prepare a short speech to present to our audience of distinguished guests.

No meals are provided during Wilderness Adventure Week. Have fun!

Monday through Friday
Wilderness Adventure Week

Saturday
Return to camp
Rehearse for Sibling Appreciation Day
Pack

Sunday
Finish packing
Sibling Appreciation Day program
Depart camp

ACTIVITIES WEEK FOUR

Only campers who failed White Glove Inspection have activities this week.

MIMI GEMS	IVAN GEMS
Polish all Harmony family memorabilia in the Harmony Hall of Fame	Mop and wax all floors (Use a toothbrush for corners)
Mow grass; trim hedges	Clean out chicken house, pig pen & barn
Clean all bathrooms	Lay new carpet in Melody Mansion
Dust all buildings	Empty garbage in all buildings
Finish painting theater in Melody Mansion	

Weather Forecast:

Temperatures in the mid-90s all week. Still no rain in the forecast. All counties in southern Missouri experiencing full-fledged drought conditions. No-burn order in effect for entire Ozark region. Fires strictly prohibited!

THIS WEEK AT THE WISTERIA CAFETERIA:

	MON	TUES	WED	THUR	FRI	SAT & SUN
B						
L						
D						

The cafeteria is closed during Wilderness Adventure Week.

A MEMO FROM
DOROTHY HARMONY

TRANS-LAKE MAIL

- Delivered by Canoe -
Lyle Splink, Postmaster

TO:	DWAYNE, DOLLY
FR:	DOROTHY
RE:	BIGGER THAN EVER

Good morning, Dwayne and Dolly (my favorite "brother" and sister)!

Did I tell you I got a call from K-NEWZ TV? They're sending their entertainment reporter to cover Sibling Appreciation Day. And a correspondent from PERSONS magazine is coming to interview me about what it's like to still be America's Favorite Soloist. (Hello, cover story!) Who said we were washed up? We're going to be bigger than ever!

So, I've been thinking: Maybe this duet deal of yours isn't such a dumb idea after all. It'll give you two a chance to perform for the kids, parents and all the reporters who will be here. Plus, it'll give me time to change costumes between sets.

Let's squeeze your song in right before my second solo. And Dwayne, don't worry about any additional duties that might come your way in the post-Lyle days. I'll make the twins do all of L's old jobs. That is, until we sell this tick-infested dive and get back on the road in our new tour bus. Just wait'll you see it!

Dorothy

♪Please note: I'm performing an afternoon concert at 1st Ozark Country Meadow Bank on Friday and I need a sound engineer to accompany me. I'd rather not use Lyle since there's a good chance he might not even be here -- knock on wood. Besides, I think one of the brats could do the job without too much risk. Dwayne, train whichever kid you think can handle it, and let me know which punk you pick.

Dr. Dwayne Harmony
Camp Happy Harmony
Harmony Hills, MO

Office Hours: By Appointment Only

NAME _Dorothy,_____ AGE _____

ADDRESS_____ DATE _____

℞ Glad to hear you came to your senses about
letting Doll and me perform a duet for Sibling
Appreciation Day.

I'll teach Ivan Gems how to run the sound sys-
tem. He's as dumb as the rest of the rugrats,
but I'm sure he can handle it. Any monkey
can hit "PLAY" on a tape recorder.

Dwayne

Refill __ times
❑ Label

SUBSTITUTION PERMITTED   DISPENSE AS WRITTEN

FORM 1322

Refill __ times
❑ Label

SUBSTITUTION PERMITTED   DISPENSE AS WRITTEN

FORM 1322

Refill __ times
❑ Label

DISPENSE AS WRITTEN

SUBSTITUTION PERMITTED

FORM 1322

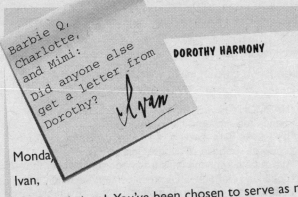

Barbie Q,
Charlotte,
and Mimi:
Did anyone else
get a letter from
Dorothy?

Ivan

DOROTHY HARMONY

Monday

Ivan,

Congratulations! You've been chosen to serve as my personal assistant at my next public appearance.

As the oldest, prettiest and most talented Harmony, I've been asked to perform some Harmony favorites at 1st Ozark Country Meadow Bank on Friday. And you'll be my sound engineer. Gee, won't that be fun?

Dwayne will teach you the ropes tomorrow night. The job isn't difficult, but it's very important. I know you can handle the responsibility, Ivan. If all goes well, maybe we'll even have you work as our sound engineer for Sibling Appreciation Day. Keep your fingers crossed!

Meet me in the Melody Mansion on Friday at 10 a.m. We'll leave for the bank from there.

Dorothy

Ivan,

None of us over here got a letter like that. Looks like it's just you and Dorothy.

Gee, won't that be ~~fun~~ creepy?

—Barbie Q.

121

PRESS RELEASE

FOR IMMEDIATE RELEASE   July 24

CONTACT: Dorothy Harmony
America's Favorite Soloist and Director of Camp Happy Harmony

AMERICA IS FALLING IN LOVE WITH THE HARMONY FAMILY, ALL OVER AGAIN!

(HARMONY HILLS, Mo.) — It was only a matter of time before America rediscovered the Harmonys.

"It's just so darn exciting," said Dorothy Harmony, the woman known as America's Favorite Soloist.

"We're getting phone calls from reporters all over the country," continued Harmony in a press conference held earlier today on the grounds of Camp Happy Harmony. "Everyone wants to know how the Harmonys are. It seems the whole nation is falling in love with our happy, harmonious family, just like they did years ago."

Reporters attending the press conference scribbled furiously as Dorothy Harmony made the following prediction:

"I think you'll be hearing a lot about us in the weeks and months to come," Dorothy said, her famous violet eyes twinkling as if on cue. "The recent interest in my family and our camp is just phenomenal."

How does the oldest, smartest and prettiest Harmony explain the Harmony renaissance?

"The people of this great country are finally waking up and realizing how important healthy, happy sibling relationships really are," Dorothy said. "And what better family to look to as an example than ours?"

Lead vocalist Dorothy Harmony and The Harmony Family Singers will perform in concert on Sunday, July 29, for a select audience of children, parents and distinguished members of the media. The program, entitled "Sibling Appreciation Day," is the culmination of a month-long course on sibling reconciliation offered at Camp Happy Harmony.

Dorothy's adoring fans can see her perform a benefit solo concert on Friday, July 27, in the main lobby of 1st Ozark Country Meadow Bank.

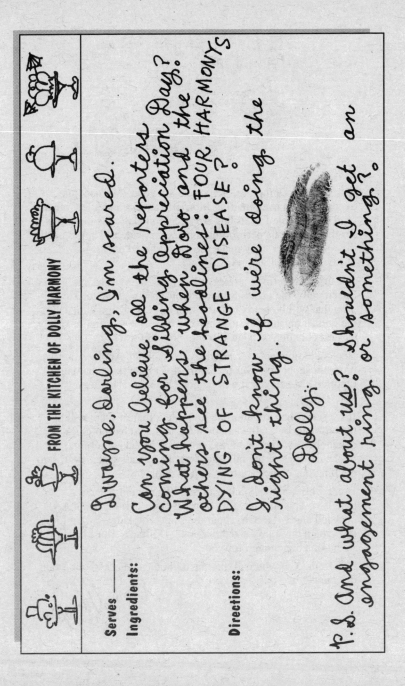

FROM THE KITCHEN OF DOLLY HARMONY

Serves ——
Ingredients:

Dwayne, darling, I'm scared.

Can you believe all the reporters
coming for Sibling Appreciation Day?
What happens when Bobo and the
others see the headlines: FOUR HARMONYS
DYING OF STRANGE DISEASE?

I don't know if we're doing the
right thing.

Dolley

Directions:

P.S. And what about us? Shouldn't I get an
engagement ring or something?

Dr. Dwayne Harmony
Nutritional Counselor

Dolly,

Don't worry, Dumpling. Reporters are good. We need the exposure. I'm even inviting Morrie Bigbucks and a few other bigwigs to come for Sibling Appreciation Day. It's important for them to get us performing together on video. They'll need the footage when they make the movie based on our lives, "The Dwayne and Dolly Story."

But first things first: strategy. I'm thinking mushrooms. Specifically, the Ozark Mountain mushroom. I've got a small crop that will be ready to harvest in time. Let's go with a simple poison mushroom stroganoff. The recipe was in one of my earliest cookbooks. Can you root around for it?

Here's the timetable for Sunday: The Sibling Appreciation Day program should be over by 6 p.m. Everyone (kids, parents, reporters, Morrie, etc.) will be gone by 6:30. That leaves just your family.

If we serve the stroganoff at 7 p.m., the four of them will be unconscious by 7:30, dead by 8:00, and cold by 9 o'clock. When the newspapers hit the streets on Monday morning, we'll be the darlings of the talk show circuit. That's when we'll start pitching our comeback tour — as a duo!

Don't worry, baby. Stick with me. We're going places — together. This time next week we'll be celebrities again AND husband and wife. Oh, about the ring. You know I want to give you a dumpling-sized diamond, Dollface. I just haven't found one big enough for you.

Gotta run. Can you call the funeral home and ask about group discounts?

XXoo Dwayne

124

CAMP-O-GRAM

Listen up, Miss Mimi.

Barbie Q. covered the entire 200 acres of camp yesterday. She must've been ridin' that burro as fast as a frog licks flies.

But here's my point. Barbie Q. says she counted 47 more trees with "Dolly Harmony + Wayne Dumbuddy = ♥ 4ever" carved into them.

Last night I snuck into the Bacteria cafeteria so I could snoop through Dolly's cookbooks. And you know what? Your brother was right! The fella who came up with those bum recipes WAS the very same Wayne Dumbuddy.

Here's his picture. I tore it off the jacket of one of his cookbooks. This Dumbuddy's no oil painting, but I reckon you might want to include him in that picture you're painting in the Melody Mansion.

Hope everything's jim-dandy with you and Ivan. I'm sending back some chow for y'all with Lyle: watercress pasta and elderberry pie.

Bone ape a teet, Miss Mimi!
(Am I spelling that right?)

Chef Brisket

Dr. Wayne Dumbuddy

CAMP-O-GRAM

TRANS-LAKE MAIL

- Delivered by Canoe -
Lyle Splink, Postmaster

Dearest Brisket,

That face!

Don't you recognize him? It's Dwayne Harmony! I'm sure of it. I've been dusting those horrible Harmony plaques and album jackets all day long. The photo from the cookbook must've been taken about 25 years ago, when the Harmonys were at the top of their game.

But why did Dr. Wayne Dumbuddy become Dwayne Harmony? Or is it the other way around? This is most bewildering.

We must ask Ivan. He's very clever at solving mysteries. He'll be able to figure all of this out.

Mimi

See? Don't they look identical?

Dwayne

Dr. Wayne Dumbuddy

CAMP-O-GRAM

Tuesday, 1:00 p.m.

Hallo, Mims.

I'm flattered you think I'm clever at solving mysteries. (Brisket gave me your last Camp-O-Gram.) And you're right. This *is* bewildering.

I've been doing a little sur-veillance around camp. I was in the Melody Mansion last night, steam cleaning the carpets. Well, that's what I was supposed to be doing, anyway. I spent most of the night trying to make sense of Dorothy Harmony's calen-dar. It's filled with cryptic notes about buying a bus, selling land, and dealing with something called *"the L situation."* I'll be honest, Mimi. I don't know what to make of all this. We need more information.

I've got to go back to the Mansion tonight from 7:00 to 8:00 so Dwayne (Harmony? Dumbuddy?) can teach me how to operate the sound equipment for Dorothy's per-formance at the bank. I won't be able to get much detective work done then, but perhaps you and I can discuss strategy (by Camp-O-Gram, that is) when I return.

Ivan

TRANS-LAKE MAIL

- Delivered by Canoe -
Lyle Splink, Postmaster

CAMP-O-GRAM

Tuesday, 2:02 p.m.

Ivan,

    If you're quite sure Dwayne's going to be gone from 7 o'clock till 8 o'clock tonight, I shall catch a ride with Lyle in his canoe over to your side of the lake. I think it's high time one of us performs a jolly good POP HIT on Dr. Dwayne's cabin.

    I'll let you know what I discover.

Mimi

TRANS-LAKE MAIL
- Delivered by Canoe -
Lyle Splink, Postmaster

 # CAMP·O·GRAM

Tuesday, 3:05 p.m.

Mimi, NO!

That's too dangerous! What if someone sees you in his cabin?

You need a look-out. And you need to be able to get away fast, in case you chance upon any of the Harmonys. I'll try to locate Barbie Q. and ask her to go with you. She'll have Sadie with her and, if need be, the two of you can make a quick escape on burroback.

But please, be careful! Believe it or not, Mimi, it would grieve me to see anything unpleasant happen to you.

Ivan

TRANS-LAKE MAIL
· Delivered by Canoe ·
Lyle Splink, Postmaster

129

CAMP-O-GRAM

Tuesday, 4:19 p.m.

Dear Ivan,

I expect you're right. Snooping through Dwayne's cabin could be dangerous. I'll wait for Barbie O. to accompany me. You're sweet to be concerned for my safety.

But you best be cautious, too. You're going to be alone with Dwayne whatever-his-last-name-is. And who knows what that wretched man is capable of? Mummy will be ever so angry with us if you die. In spite of all the things I've said in the past, I wouldn't want anything bad to happen to you either. (Not until we solve this beastly mystery, anyway!)

Mimi

TRANS-LAKE MAIL
~ Delivered by Canoe ~
Lyle Splink, Postmaster

You

WISTERIA CAFETERIA

COOKIN' WITH DOLLY

Dwayne darling,

I've searched high and low for your stroganoff recipe.
I don't have it. You must have misplaced it in your
cabin, schnookums.

Dolly

Dr. Dwayne Harmony
Camp Happy Harmony
Harmony Hills, MO

Office Hours: By Appointment Only

NAME _Delicious Dollykins,_

ADDRESS _____ AGE ___

DATE ___

℞

Please remember: I am a doctor. I
do not "misplace" things. Look
harder, Dumpling. I'm sure you'll
find the recipe.

Refill ___ times

☐ Label

xo Dwayne

SUBSTITUTION PERMITTED   DISPENSE AS WRITTEN

FORM 1322

WISTERIA CAFETERIA

COOKIN' WITH DOLLY

Dwayne,

I don't know what to make of your last note. Do you think you are incapable of mis- placing things just because you're a doctor, whereas I, with my diploma from Miss Tammy Sue's Junior College, am more prone to ~~errores~~ ~~misstakes~~ goof-ups? (Forget that last part.)

I don't *have* the recipe for your stupid mushroom stroganoff. Maybe you should call that little tart you hired back when you were writing your cookbooks. What was her name? Boopsie? Boom Boom? Seems to me she did more than her share of the work on those books. But then again, you've always had a knack for finding talented women and riding their coattails to success.

Ringless still,

Dolly

Dr. Dwayne Harmony
Camp Happy Harmony
Harmony Hills, MO

Office Hours: By Appointment Only

NAME __Dolly, baby, please.__ AGE _____

ADDRESS _____ DATE _____

℞ How many times do I have to tell you? Bambi and I were just friends. If it makes you feel any better, I'll run into town right now and pick up a marriage license from the courthouse. Will for- ward to you via Trans-Lake Mail.

Forget about finding the recipe. I'm sure I can recreate the stroganoff from memory.

Yours only,

Dwayne

Refill __times
❑ Label

SUBSTITUTION PERMITTED   DISPENSE AS WRITTEN

FORM 1322

MARRIAGE LICENSE

NAME OF BRIDE

CAMP-O-GRAM

ALMOST MIDNIGHT, TUESDAY NIGHT

CHARLOTTE,

HOLD ON TO YOUR YOKE, COWPOKE!

YOU FLAT WON'T BELIEVE WHAT MIMI AND I
FOUND IN DWAYNE'S CABIN. SEE FOR YOUR-
SELF. IT HURTS MY BRAIN JUST TO THINK
ABOUT IT.

I'M GIVING IT TO LYLE TO DELIVER SO YOU CAN
HIDE IT IN THE WOODS. I GOTTA RIDE MIMI BACK
TO HER CABIN BEFORE THOSE LOUSY HARMONY
BROADS WAKE UP.

I'M TELLING YOU – WHEN IT COMES TO THIS
HARMONY BUSINESS, THE MORE YOU STIR IT,
THE MORE IT STINKS.

- BARBIE Q.

TRANS-LAKE MAIL
· Delivered by Canoe ·
Lyle Splink, Postmaster

MARRIAGE LICENSE

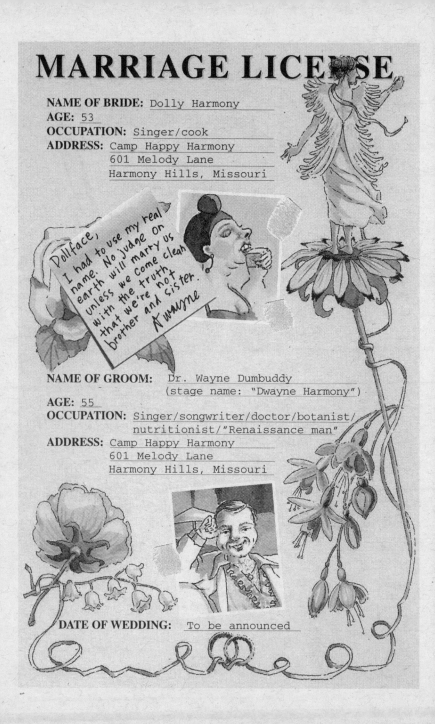

NAME OF BRIDE: Dolly Harmony

AGE: 53

OCCUPATION: Singer/cook

ADDRESS: Camp Happy Harmony
601 Melody Lane
Harmony Hills, Missouri

Dollface,
I had to use my real name. No judge on earth will marry us unless we come clean with the truth, that we're not brother and sister.
Dwayne

NAME OF GROOM: Dr. Wayne Dumbuddy
(stage name: "Dwayne Harmony")

AGE: 55

OCCUPATION: Singer/songwriter/doctor/botanist/
nutritionist/"Renaissance man"

ADDRESS: Camp Happy Harmony
601 Melody Lane
Harmony Hills, Missouri

DATE OF WEDDING: To be announced

CAMP-O-GRAM

TRANS-LAKE MAIL
- Delivered by Canoe -
Lyle Splink, Postmaster

Wednesday, 2:07 a.m.

Dear Mimi,

!!!!!

That's the sound of me screaming. I don't know which is more bizarre:

1. that Dolly and Dwayne are not brother and sister, or

2. that Dwayne Harmony is really Wayne Dumbuddy, or

3. that Dolly and Dwayne (or should I say Wayne?) are getting married!

Any way you look at it, it's too weird!

I just told Ivan about it. He says you're painting Dwayne Harmony with two faces in your mural. Perfect! Ivan also said he got some very strange instructions last night from Dwayne about how to operate the sound equipment for Dorothy's concert at the bank. Ivan didn't really go into details. Just said something about the pieces of the puzzle starting to come together. (Maybe for him. I'm still confused!)

Anyway, Charlie and I are going to conduct a White Glove Inspection in Dorothy's office later today, while she's rehearsing. If we find anything, we'll let you guys know.

Everything's OK out here in the woods. Brisket's holding down the fort and cooking for us. Try this persimmon pastry. Isn't it delicious? Lyle says it's the best food he's ever tasted!

Talk to you soon.

Charlotte

Dearest Charlotte,

       The persimmon pastry was scrumptious, but these Harmonys are absolutely foul. This is turning out to be a first-class mystery, not to mention splendid material for my mural.

       Speaking of the mural, I seem to have hit a creative roadblock. I very much wish to paint Dwayne Harmony's portrait with two faces (since he is a despicable two-faced brute), but I'm not sure which pictures to use as my models. The man's profile has changed so dramatically over the years. In some photographs, he looks exactly like the cookbook author, Dr. Wayne Dumbuddy. See what I mean?

But in other photographs, especially the older pictures of
The Harmony Family Singers, Dwayne doesn't look anything like
Dumbuddy. He doesn't even look like Dwayne. Don't you agree?

This IS a puzzle, isn't it?

Miss you,
Mimi

TRANS-LAKE MAIL
- Delivered by Canoe -
Lyle Splink, Postmaster

Dwayne,

I'm still waiting to see a marriage license, Doctor. Do you keep all your patients waiting this long? No wonder you have so few.

Sign me,
Losing MY patience* on this side of the lake. *Dolley*

*You're not the only one around here with a quick wit, Mr. Big Shot.

Dolly baby,

You're not going to believe this, Dumpling, but I can't find the marriage license. I picked it up yesterday. Now I can't find it anywhere.

Dwayne

Dwayne:

Can't find the marriage license? Imagine that. Maybe it ran away with the mushroom stroganoff recipe.

You and your excuses . . . . Some doctor you are. You make me sick.

Dolley

Dollface,

Please, let's not argue. I'll get another marriage license next week AND a ring. I promise. For now, we must stay focused on the issue at hand: Stroganoff. I'll be in the kitchen tonight measuring ingredients. Stop by if you want to talk, etc.

Xo? *Dwayne*

138

DATE **Wednesday** HOUR 2:00 p.m.

TO ~~Dale and Daryl~~

WHILE YOU WERE OUT

M ME

OF

PHONE

☐ Telephoned ☐ Returned Call ☐ Left Package
☐ Please Call ☒ Was In ☒ Please See Me!
☐ Will Call Again ☐ Won't Call ☒ Important

MESSAGE:

Well ????? We're more than halfway through Wilderness Adventure Week and Lyle is still here. What's your excuse this time?

SIGNED **Dorothy**

DA TWINS

Relax, Doro.

We're sharpening our arrows even as we write these words. Target practice is ~~skedjeweled for~~ tomorrow (Thurzday) night.

Your bulls-eye brothers,

Dale

Daryl

About time. Let me know when the deed is done.
Dorothy

TRANS-LAKE MAIL
- Delivered by Canoe -
Lyle Splink, Postmaster

CAMP-O-GRAM

Ivan,

Charlotte and I just conducted our own White Glove Inspection in the Melody Mansion. Guess what we found in Dorothy's office? Charlotte's camera. Now we can finally start getting some photos of all the weirdness around here.

And take a look at what we found in an envelope labeled "SECRET" in Dorothy's file cabinet. It's an agreement made 25 years ago between Lyle and Dorothy Harmony. Can you make any sense of it?

W.B.F. (Write back fast)

TRANS-LAKE MAIL
- Delivered by Canoe -
Lyle Splink, Postmaster

Charlie

AGREEMENT

THIS INDENTURE, made between

Lyle Harmony

and

Dorothy Harmony

(acting on behalf of herself and Dolly, Darlene, Daryl, Dale Harmony and Dr. Wayne Dumbuddy),

Witnesseth that

Lyle Harmony

For and in consideration of

NEVER TELLING THE HARMONY FAMILY SECRETS

Shall be the

SOLE OWNER

Of all
Harmony Family Real Estate

As part of this Agreement, from this date forward, Lyle Harmony shall legally adopt the name

Lyle Splink

IN WITNESS WHEREOF, the said parties have hereunto set their hands.

Dorothy Harmony

Dorothy Harmony
(acting on behalf of herself, her above-named siblings and Dr. Wayne Dumbuddy)

Lyle Harmony

Lyle Harmony
(known hence forward as Lyle Splink)

Camp Happy Harmony

Charlie,

Have Charlotte show you how to
illuminate this letter. It was
typewritten with invisible ink.

TRANS-LAKE MAIL · Delivered by

Charlie,

   If what the Agreement says is true,
Lyle is actually a Harmony brother.

   I find this almost impossible to
believe, but there's only one way to
find out. Someone's got to ask Lyle.
I think Brisket is our man. Lyle's
become a big fan of his cooking. And
you know how those two like to talk
after dinner.

   I'll give the Agreement to Barbie
Q. to deliver to Brisket. Did you
know she taught Sadie to cross the
lake? Such a clever gal, that Barbie
Q.! I suggest we send all communication about Lyle via Barbie Q.'s burro
service — just in case Lyle really is
related to the rest of those rotten
Harmony eggs.

   A messy affair, this.

                              Ivan

P.S. Delighted to hear Charlotte
reclaimed her camera! Good show!

143

WISTERIA CAFETERIA

COOKIN' WITH DOLLY

Dear Dwayney-kins,

Last night was wonderful. I'm so glad I stopped by. Cooking with you, even if it's a deadly stroganoff, is always magic for me. I live for the day we can make beautiful music together on stage and at home, as husband and wife.

And I'm sorry I've been so moody lately. As you can imagine, what we're about to do to my family makes me a little uneasy. But you were right when you said you can't choose your relatives. You can only choose to get rid of them.

I've stored the stroganoff in the freezer. We'll thaw and serve on Sunday evening.

With love,

The (almost) Mrs. Wayne Dumbuddy

or

Dolly Dumbuddy

or

Dolly Harmony-Dumbuddy

or

Dolly Harmuddy (that's Harmony + Dumbuddy)

Which one do you like best, dear?

CAMP-O-GRAM

Thursday, 9:20 a.m.

Brisket,

Charlotte and Charlie found this Agreement in Dorothy's office. I think you'd best hide it in the woods for safekeeping. I also think you better schedule a chat with Lyle to find out what these Harmony Secrets are all about.

If I read the Agreement correctly, it says that Lyle is actually a Harmony. I can't believe this is true. But notice what the Agreement says about Lyle changing his name. It also appears that Lyle owns Camp Happy Harmony.

Would you please see what you can find out about this matter?

I'm off to the bank with Dorothy tomorrow. I'm her new "sound boy," as she calls me. I'd object to the moniker, but I'm hoping the torture of spending time with her will result in the discovery of more clues.

Here's to luck on both our missions.

Ivan

P.S. Barbie Q. just delivered today's breakfast: potato fritatta with peach chutney. Bravo! As your sister said, you've become the hideaway gourmet. Well done!

CAMP-O-GRAM

After lunch on Thursday

Ivan,

Well, I chewed the fat with Lyle, just like you asked. And I don't mind telling you, it was stranger than a three-legged hound in high heels.

Here's what happened. I made a big old skillet of corn bread. It's Lyle's favorite lunch. Barbie Q.'s, too. (Did she really say I was a gourmet? Hot tamale! That's the first nice thing my sister's EVER said about me.)

Back to my story. So Lyle and I are at the campsite, tearing off hunks of corn bread and dipping 'em in the apple butter I made the night before last. Lyle said he'd give his false teeth to know how to make apple butter like I do.

That's when I took the Agreement out of my pocket, real dramatic-like. I said I'd teach him how to make apple butter AND fried huckleberry pie if he'd tell me what the dancin' donkeys THIS was all about. (I was holding the Agreement right in front of his eyeballs when I said that last part.)

Well, Lyle got real quiet. Wouldn't say boo. Then I asked him if he ever changed his name. No answer. Then I asked him if he was kin to those stinkin', rotten', bad-as-three-year-old-headcheese Harmonys. Lyle commenced to sniffle a little and said he couldn't tell.

I didn't push him after that. Kickin' never gets you nowheres, unless you're a mule. I reckon we better take this investigation real slow and steady, Ivan. Like we say on the ranch, the only fast way to drive cattle is slow.

Move 'em out!

Brisket

P.S. I'm sending along some hush puppies for you to stick in your ears when Dorothy sings at the bank. I'm not missing that Harmony music one iota. Charlie's been keeping us plenty entertained out here with the songs he's writing. He's dang good.

K-NEWZ TV

NEWS AT NOON
with
Harry and Bunny

T R A N S C R I P T
July 27

BUNNY: Welcome to News at Noon. The top story today is a sad tale, indeed. Our man Harry is on the scene in Harmony Hills, Missouri. Harry, what can you tell us?

HARRY: Thank you, Bunny. I'm standing here in the foyer of 1st Ozark Country Meadow Bank. In the background you can see Dorothy Harmony performing for patrons of the bank. Dorothy is the most famous member of The Harmony Family Singers, those beloved brothers and sisters who, by their harmonious example of sibling love, won the hearts of families everywhere.

BUNNY: But the Harmonys are singing a sadder tune these days. Isn't that right, Harry?

HARRY: I'm afraid so, Bunny. Though the family has not discussed this publicly, we know from reliable sources in the music industry that four Harmonys — Dale, Daryl, Darlene and Dorothy — have been diagnosed with the mysterious and fatal illness known as Ozark Mountain Cabin Fever. But in the true spirit of Harmony, these talented singers are smiling all the way to the grave. Right now, Dorothy is singing her brains out as usual. And on Sunday night, the entire Harmony family will give what might be their last public performance together at Sibling Appreciation Day.

BUNNY: Oh, it just breaks my heart, Harry. What's the mood like there at the bank?

HARRY: Bunny, the scene here is absolutely gutwrenching. If you didn't know better, you'd think nothing was wrong with Dorothy Harmony. She's her usual bubbly self. And her voice is... well, it's uncanny. She sounds EXACTLY like she did 30 years ago.

BUNNY: Dorothy is not letting this Ozark Mountain Cabin Fever bug get her down, is she, Harry?

HARRY: No siree, Bunny. In fact, she and her siblings are planning a major comeback this fall. I have the president of 1st Ozark Country Meadow Bank standing by with details. Sir, can you tell us what you know of the Harmonys' plans for the future?

BANK PRESIDENT: All I know is that Dorothy's borrowed a heckuva lot of money in the last couple of weeks. Says she's buying a new tour bus for The Harmony Family Singers so they can take their show on the road again. I didn't know a thing about this Ozark Mountain Cabin Fever business until just now. If I did . . . Well, I don't know that we could've made those loans to Miss Harmony. I mean, she's a nice enough old gal. But like I said, she's up to her eyeballs in debt. She used that camp they've got out there as collateral. Said she wanted to sell the old place as soon as she could and just travel around the country, singing and staying in fancy schmancy hotels like they used to when they were real famous.

HARRY: Well, it's an inspiration to us all that this family can look death in the face and continue to make plans for the future. Back to you, Bunny.

BUNNY: What a story, Harry. We'll look forward to your follow-up report on Sunday. And now, more about Ozark Mountain Cabin Fever, an illness so rare that our medical experts have been unable to find any other case studies of people who have fallen prey to this silent killer.

CAMP·O·GRAM

Brisket,

I write in great haste, every minute being precious.

I've just returned from the bank with Dorothy. I think I know her secret, but I have no proof. I must watch some of the videotapes of their old TV show to see for certain if my theory is correct. It seems that . . . Well, I shan't jump to conclusions. Let's just say I think Dorothy's a fake — and in more ways than one.

In the meantime, my real concern is Lyle. I have reason to believe he might be in danger. I overheard Dorothy talking to some of the loan officers at the bank. From the sounds of it, she's recently borrowed a tidy sum of money against the camp with the intention to sell the property soon. I don't know how she could sell the camp if, as the Agreement indicated, Lyle owns it. Unless . . . Unless she plans to get rid of Lyle.

This could be serious. You may want to suggest to Lyle that he camp out with you and the others in the woods, just in case those fiendish Harmonys (Lyle excluded) are capable of murder.

Please be careful, Brisket. And tell Barbie Q., Charlie and Charlotte the same. I don't know what I'd do if any harm came to my best friends in the whole world.

I'll let you know what I find after reviewing the tapes from the Harmonys' old TV show.

On the Harmony trail,

I am,

Inspector Ivan

TRANS-LAKE MAIL · Delivered by Burro Service

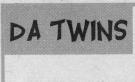

DA TWINS

— HAND DELIVERED —

~~Fryday~~ Friday

Doro,

Mission accomplished.

We got him last night. It was ~~reel~~
real dark, but we heard his last cry.
    Here's the bow that launched
     the winning shot.
     Thought you might
        like to bronze it for a
              ~~soovanear~~ trophy.

        Guess now that Lyle's gone,
      we're stuck delivering our own
       mail. Oh well. Small price to
       pay for offing the L man. Now
       let's sell this funny farm and get
       the heck out of here.

                    Dale ~~L~~ and Daryl

CAMP·O·GRAM

Ivan,

You were worried the Harmonys might be *capable of murder?* Those worthless weasels tried to COMMIT MURDER last night! It was like this:

Charlotte, Charlie, Lyle, Brisket and me were eating catfish in our usual spot in the orchard. After supper I tried to talk Lyle into camping out with us. He wouldn't. Said he was too old and tired to sleep in the woods. So he went back to his cabin while the rest of us stayed up to talk and dance.

Brisket was baking a peanut butter and chocolate cake on the grill. (Lyle got the p.b. and chocolate for us from town.) The cake turned out dang-near delicious. You shoulda seen us eatin' it. We looked like a bunch of wasps around a honey pot.

Well, knowing how much Lyle likes sweets, we reckoned we oughta take him a piece of cake. I told Charlotte to cut a big old slab and jump on the back of Sadie. Then I rode both of us over to Lyle's cabin.

Just as we were getting close, we spied Dale and Daryl standing outside Lyle's window. They each had a bow and arrows and were aiming directly at Lyle!

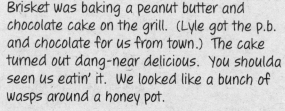

152

Luckily, those muleheads missed -- probably 'cause I yelled like a stuck pig and scared 'em silly. They took off running and never looked back.

Lyle's OK. He's just rattled by the whole thing. (And who the pickled pig's ears wouldn't be?) Daryl and Dale didn't see us watching the whole show from the woods. But Charlotte pulled out her camera — cobra-quick! — and snapped some pictures of those crummy Harmony twins in the act.

We're going to develop the film tomorrow. Brisket says he knows how. (Who knew my brother was such a brain?) In the meantime, Lyle is staying with us for his protection.

But Ivan, how much more evidence do we need to prove what we've known all along? These Harmonys (not counting Lyle) are the low-downest bunch of horses' behinds ever created! I say we stuff and mount 'em all.

- Barbie Q.

TRANS-LAKE MAIL • Delivered by Burro Service

Barbie Q., Brisket, Charlie and Charlotte:

THOSE SCOUNDRELS!

You're right, Barbie Q. With the exception of Lyle, the Harmonys ARE a despicable bunch of hooligans.

I've just finished scanning countless episodes of the old "Harmony Begins At Home" TV show on videotape in the Melody Mansion. My suspicions were confirmed. Dorothy Harmony IS a fraud. I'll tell you all about her shenanigans when you return tomorrow.

And if you thought Dale and Daryl were monsters for trying to kill Lyle, listen to this: Dwayne and Dolly have plans to poison those two rogues, *plus* Darlene and Dorothy, on Sunday! I finally got around to emptying the garbage (one of my chores for the week) and found in the trash a whole slew of letters written by Dwayne and Dolly, outlining their nefarious scheme. It's check-mate in this Harmony game!

Now that we've unraveled the Harmony family's web of deceit, we need a strategy for exposing them. I vote for Sibling Appreciation Day. All our parents will be here, plus scads of reporters.

For my part, I shall row across the lake to tell Mimi of my findings and hear her ideas for how best to unmask the sinister charade that is the Harmony family.

Onward, brave campers!

CAMP-O-GRAM

TRANS-LAKE MAIL
Delivered by Burro Service

Dearest Barbie Q. and Charlotte,

The twins tried to kill Lyle?? Those vulgar villains! Ivan told me the whole story. I'm simply relieved to hear you're both safe and well. As you might imagine, I'm redesigning the entire mural in the Melody Mansion. We want to paint a true portrait of these loathsome Harmonys, do we not?

Have you the stomachs for yet another ally-oop on this rollercoaster ride? If so, read on.

When Ivan came over to see me earlier today, I was in the Melody Mansion. I had just started to paint one of the higher sections on the east wall of the theater and I needed something to stand on.

So, with the intention to borrow a chair, Ivan and I crept into Dorothy's office. You can't imagine what we found. I could scarcely believe my eyes. Sitting right in the middle of Dorothy's desk was a stack of form letters she's been sending to our parents with OUR signatures forged on them! I rather think we should title our mural "The Harmony Hall of Shame."

Well, I best sign off so I can get back to my painting. I do hope I finish in time. I'm keeping

the mural under wraps behind a velvet curtain. On Sunday
we shall give new meaning to the word "unveiling."

I look forward to seeing you, dears, when you and
your brothers return tomorrow.

Missing you all,

Mimi

CAMP-O-GRAM

Dear Mimi,

You're right about that form letter business taking the cake. Well, almost . . . . You know how we thought all our parents had forgotten about us since we hadn't heard from them? Turns out they've been writing to us all along.

We found a huge barrel at Lyle's filled with our REAL letters. Lyle was supposed to be burning all this stuff, but he hasn't because it's been so dry. He hadn't even looked in the barrel for more than a month.

What this means is more proof for us. And real food, too, because guess what else we found in the barrel -- SIX boxes filled with tons of food! Barbie Q. and Brisket's dad has been sending them care packages from Texas every week. The boxes were sealed really tight, so all the food is still good.

You should hear the song my brother's writing for us to sing at Sibling Appreciation Day. It's all about the Harmonys. I'm making up a dance to go with it. Barbie Q.'s making costumes for us to wear. And Brisket's cooking a bunch of food to serve our parents after the program. Even Lyle's getting in on the act. Wait till you see him dance! We're keeping him hidden until tomorrow, though, so those low-life twins don't use him for target practice again.

We'll be back soon to teach you and Ivan the song and dance steps. This is going to be fun!

Charlotte

P.S. Check out these pictures. Thought you might want to include this scene in the mural. And don't worry about finishing it on time. Barbie Q. and I can help you when we get back. I can't wait to see it — and you!

Week
of

Camp Happy Harmony
SIBLING APPRECIATION DAY
July 29
Program

Welcome to our happy home!............................Dorothy Harmony

Opening solo ....Dorothy Harmony
"O Sibling Mio"

Duet...Dolly and Dwayne Harmony
"Love Denied Makes the Turtledoves Cry"

Solo...Dorothy Harmony
"The Oldest Sibling Knows (Right Down to Her Toes)"

Sibling presentations:

"What I Learned At Camp Happy Harmony"
Mimi and Ivan Gems
Charlotte and Charlie Lee
Barbie Q. and Brisket Roast

Grand unveiling of Melody Mansion mural..................Mimi Gems

Finale.........................Harmony Family Singers and All Campers
"We'd Rather Sing Than Fight, 'Cause Being Polite Is Such A Delight"

Dismissal

☐ Sell Camp.
☐ Send final payment to
 Beautiful Buses.
☐ ~~Work on badges~~
☐ Hire accountant (+ lawyer?
☐ Buy paper shredder.

K-NEWZ TV

LIVE AT FIVE
with
Harry and Bunny

TRANSCRIPT
July 29

BUNNY: Good evening and welcome to Live at Five. Tonight's top story is going to be a tearjerker for a lot of people who grew up with the sweet sounds of The Harmony Family Singers. Our man Harry is on the scene in Harmony Hills, Missouri with an exclusive report. Harry, what can you tell us?

HARRY: Thank you, Bunny. I'm standing on the steps of the Melody Mansion on what must be a bittersweet night for the world-famous Harmony Family Singers, four of whom have been diagnosed with the fatal disease known as Ozark Mountain Cabin Fever. Tonight the Harmonys are giving what might be their final performance together at an event they call simply Sibling Appreciation Day.

BUNNY: Isn't that fitting, Harry, for a family that has devoted its entire career to singing the joys of sibling love? What's the mood like there at the mansion?

HARRY: Well, Bunny, leave it to the Harmonys to put on a happy face. This place is thick with reporters from around the world. To be honest, many of us are having a difficult time holding back the tears. But I haven't seen a single tear from the Harmonys themselves. The sisters look as beautiful as ever, and the brothers appear surprisingly robust. It's just a testament to their strength and courage that they're able to hold their heads high and maintain such composure during this difficult time.

BUNNY: What about Dwayne and Dolly, the two Harmonys not afflicted with the deadly Ozark Mountain Cabin Fever? This must be an agonizing time for them, Harry.

HARRY: You got that right, Bunny. And that's the interesting thing here. If I had to say which Harmony looked the worst, it would have to be Dolly. She has a disturbed, even faraway look in her eyes. Clearly, she's more distressed than either of her two sisters. Dwayne is the only other Harmony who, thus far, has escaped the deadly wrath of this brutal disease. And he too looks as if he hasn't had a good night's sleep since his brothers and sisters were diagnosed. Industry insiders tell us that Dolly and Dwayne are caring for the other four Harmonys during their final days.

BUNNY: Just imagine what these last few weeks have been like for those two as they contemplate their future together. Harry, can we safely say Dolly and Dwayne's singing career is over?

HARRY: Absolutely. There's no question about that, Bunny. In fact, Dolly and Dwayne just performed a duet number that completely bombed.

BUNNY: How can two lonely voices ever replace the sound of six happy Harmonys singing as one?

HARRY: Good point, Bunny. And speak of the devil! Look who just stepped outside the mansion for a breath of fresh air. Dolly Harmony! Ms. Harmony, can you tell us how it feels to know your brothers and sisters are not long for this world?

DOLLY: Well . . . Um . . . Er . . . You know, that darn Ozark Mountain Cabin Fever is such a rascal. It really is a cruel disease. I hope one day we can find a cure for it. I . . . I . . . I have to go now.

HARRY: Thank you, Dolly. Back to you, Bunny.

BUNNY: (Sniffle, sniffle) That was beautiful. Thank you, Harry. We'll check back in with you later in the broadcast. Now, let's go live to the stage of the Melody Mansion where Dorothy Harmony, America's Favorite Soloist, is performing her second number of the evening, and one of my personal favorites, "The Oldest Sibling Knows (Right Down To Her Toes)."

DOROTHY HARMONY: (singing on stage)

As the oldest sibling
In a family of offspring,
Let me share with you
A family clue or two.

(Refrain)
Because the oldest sibling knows
Right down to her toes,
There can be no tears or woes
When love between siblings grows.

I'm pretty and I'm wise;
I'm so petite in size.

And the birds ·join with me in song
So *why don't you sing alo--*
(SCCRREEEEECCHHH)

So why don't you sing alon--
(SCCRRAAAAATCCCHHH)

What are you doing, Ivan? Turn that tape
recorder back on! NOW!

BUNNY: Harry, what's going on? We can't
hear the music.

HARRY: This is very strange, Bunny.
Dorothy Harmony abruptly ended her song mid-
verse with an ear-splitting scream and then
ran off the stage.· If I'm not mistaken, she
was using language we don't normally associ-
ate with The Harmony Family Singers.

BUNNY: A symptom of Ozark Mountain Cabin
Fever, perhaps?

HARRY: Very possibly. Just a moment.
What's this? Some kids are taking the
stage. I'm told . . . Is that right? It
seems these children are the campers who
have spent the past month here at Camp Happy
Harmony. We're told they've prepared a
statement of some kind about what they've
learned here. Let's have a listen.

CAMPERS: (singing on stage)

They say they're siblings, it's true,
But have we got news for you.
They're not smart, sweet kids
And you should see·them flip their lids.

You see, we've spent four weeks
Living with these Harmony freaks.
And by our work as spies and sleuths
We've uncovered some terrible truths.

Like the fact that,

(Refrain)
They'd rather scam than work
'Cause they're all a bunch of jerks.
It may sound callous and mean
Until you hear about the cuisine.

It's not that the food served on their dishes
Was simply bad or non-nutritious.
It was that and even more,
For their kitchen was like a drugstore.

They added ingredients to our food
That can change a person's mood.
Lucky for us no one died
At the hands of these Jekyll and Hydes.

HARRY: Bunny, I have to break in here for a moment and tell you this performance has taken an amazing and completely unexpected turn. The children on stage are telling a jaw-dropping story about the Harmony family. Security guards have moved in and restrained some members of the family who apparently tried to flee the scene. Dorothy Harmony has been handcuffed. Dolly Harmony is sweating like a chunk of rotten pork. And now, a velvet curtain has been pulled to reveal a mural that . . . Can you hear the gasps from the audience, Bunny?

BUNNY: Yes, I can. Can we get a camera on the mural, please? Harry, what's this all about?

HARRY: Bunny, I'm told the young campers designed this very sophisticated work of art, which seems to tell a story of some kind. Let's have a look at this extraordinary painting as this compelling drama literally unfolds before our very eyes.

THE MAIN STREET JOURNAL

July 30   50 cents

HARMONY FAMILY CRIME RING BROKEN

Harmony Family Singers Booked on Charges of Lip-Synching, Bank Fraud, Attempted Murder

HARMONY HILLS, Mo. - A dramatic undercover investigation conducted by six summer campers landed The Harmony Family Singers in jail last night.

Lead singer Dorothy Harmony, known to millions of fans as "America's Favorite Soloist," was booked on charges of felony lip-synching, bank fraud, and plotting to murder Lyle Splink, a soft-spoken mail carrier who is, in fact, the eldest Harmony brother.

Middle sister Dolly Harmony was charged with conspiring to poison her siblings with a deadly mushroom stroganoff. Also charged in connection with the stroganoff scheme was Dr. Wayne Dumbuddy, a man who for years has posed as a Harmony sibling.

Under direct questioning at police headquarters last night, Dumbuddy admitted that he is not a Harmony. Rather, he was simply a next-door neighbor of the Harmony family who was hired by Dorothy Harmony to join the act when Lyle quit the group.

Harmony family and Wayne Dumbuddy in police custody

Twins Dale and Daryl Harmony were charged with the attempted murder of Lyle (Splink) Harmony, as ordered by Dorothy. The twins were also charged with poisoning Lyle's dog, Jazz. Darlene Harmony was charged with crimes against fashion.

The Harmony crime ring was exposed during a compelling presentation at the Melody Mansion. As the campers explained in song the inner workings of The Harmony Family Singers, a curtain was pulled to reveal an original mural which illustrated the elaborate schemes that almost resulted in Lyle's death.

The Harmony Family Singers will be held without bail in the Harmony Hills County Jail while they await their day in court. Dorothy Harmony's request to perform concerts for her fellow inmates as a way of repaying her bank loans has been denied by the judge, who feared mass riots.

Kids Provide Links in Harmony Hijinx
Who are these kids? Why were they here?

HARMONY HILLS, Mo. - Who then are the six children who busted the Harmony family crime ring? Their names are: Mimi and Ivan Gems, Charlotte and Charlie Lee, and Barbie Q. and Brisket Roast.

All six children were enrolled at Camp Happy Harmony in a four-week course designed to improve their sibling relationships.

But as Barbie Q. Roast of Porterhouse, Texas put it: "That was all a bunch of half-baked hogwash."

Her twin brother, Brisket Roast, agreed. "Barbie Q.'s right. Those

(Continued on page 2, column 1)

Brisket Roast

Barbie Q. Roast

Ivan Gems

Mimi Gems

Charlie Lee

Charlotte Lee

(From page 1)

Harmonys would rather climb a tree and lie than stand here and tell you the truth. Fact is, they didn't teach us beans. They just made us do all the dadblamed work around this place. And you should've seen the slop they tried to feed us!"

Charlotte and Charlie Lee, both from Stopsign, Ill., concurred with the Roasts on all points except one. "Well, we did learn some stuff from one of the Harmonys," Charlie Lee said. "Lyle taught me how to write music."

Lyle (Splink) Harmony was also the inspiration for an original dance choreographed by Charlotte Lee and performed by the campers during last night's presentation.

All six campers agreed that Lyle is the only member of the Harmony family who is innocent of criminal activity.

"We have all the paperwork and a beautiful mural to show that Lyle is completely blameless in his brothers' and sisters' crimes," Ivan Gems of London, England told reporters.

Ivan's sister, Mimi, agreed with her brother. "Lyle is a very dear man who was wronged by his brothers and sisters," Miss Gems stated. "It's a pity, really. I'm just glad we were able to solve this case and expose the rest of the Harmonys as the wicked people they are."

An emotional Lyle (Splink) Harmony thanked the children for their work in the investigation.

"These kids saved my life," Lyle said, choking back tears.

Then, in a touching scene straight out of Hollywood, the six campers presented Lyle with his fully-recovered dog, Jazz.

"We found an antidote for the poison in one of Dumbuddy's cookbooks," explained Barbie Q. Roast, who delivered the recipe by burro-back to a local veterinary clinic where Jazz was being treated.

The cookbook, no longer in print, is titled "Reverse the Curse: Antidotes to Live By." It was written by Wayne and Bambi Dumbuddy.

Forensic Report Concludes
Stroganoff *Was* Deadly

WASHINGTON - The kids were right.

The mushroom stroganoff which Dolly Harmony and Wayne Dumbuddy (a.k.a. Dwayne Harmony) had planned to serve members of the Harmony family last night was poisonous.

Dr. Todd Stool at the U.S. Sporatorium in Washington, D.C. studied the stroganoff and confirmed the campers' allegations.

"Anyone who ate that stroganoff would have been dead within the hour," Dr. Stool said.

Or as Brisket Roast put it: "The proof of the pudding is in the stroganoff."

And what about Ozark Mountain Cabin Fever?

"No such thing," sniffed Dr. Stool. "If I had to guess, I'd say Dolly and Dumbuddy simply made it up to explain what they hoped would be a quick and clean quadruple murder."

According to chief investigator Ivan Gems, co-conspirators Dolly Harmony and Wayne Dumbuddy deserve nothing less than "the business end of a falling piano."

K-NEWZ TV

NEWS AT NOON
with
Harry and Bunny

T R A N S C R I P T
July 30

BUNNY: Good day. Well, there's no need to tell you what today's top story is. The Stroganoff Scandal. The Lip-Synch Fink. Call it what you will, the whole country's talking about the Harmony family crime ring and the kids who cracked the case. Our man Harry is on the scene in Harmony Hills, Missouri. Harry, will you introduce us to the young heroes?

HARRY: Bunny, it would be my great honor to introduce you and all of our viewers to Mimi and Ivan Gems, Charlotte and Charlie Lee, Barbie Q. and Brisket Roast.

BUNNY: Kids, this must be an exciting day for you. I hear the mayor of Harmony Hills has planned a parade in your honor. What do you think of all this attention?

(Silence)

BUNNY: Hello? Harry? Kids? Can you hear me?

HARRY: We can hear you all right. Our heroes appear to be a little shy. Is that true, kids?

CHARLIE: (softly) Ivan, you tell him.

IVAN: Well, to be perfectly honest, though we're honored by all the fanfare, it's rather a sad day for us.

HARRY: Sad? Why's that?

CHARLOTTE: Because after it's over, we have to leave.

BUNNY: So I take it you've all become friends through this harrowing ordeal?

BRISKET: 'Course we have! And jumpin' jingle bells, it wasn't no harrowin' ordeal. Fact is, it was kinda fun.

HARRY: Fun?! You kids could've been killed.

170

MIMI: You're quite right. But the truth is, we did a most respectable job watching out for one another.

BUNNY: But children, weren't you scared?

BARBIE Q.: Listen lady, do we look like a bunch of scaredy-pants? Besides, most of the time we were too busy laughing to be scared.

MIMI: Indeed, after a full day of chores, we spent many an hour aching with fatigue but laughing uproariously at the absurdity of those Harmony blokes.

HARRY: Huh?

BARBIE Q.: That's just how Mimi talks. She can't help using all those toe-tappin' words. What she's saying is we were busy as a band of one-armed paper hangers working for those lousy Harmonys, who are a bunch of cow patties-for-craniums.

HARRY: Oh, I see.

CHARLOTTE: Charlie was always cracking us up with his songs.

IVAN: And Charlotte taught us to dance.

CHARLIE: Brisket cooked all our food for us.

BARBIE Q.: And Mimi gave us painting lessons.

BRISKET: Ivan here put all the pieces of the mystery together.

MIMI: And Barbie Q. created these charming frocks for us to wear and delivered our mail when Lyle couldn't.

BUNNY: Speaking of Lyle, where is he?

HARRY: He's right here, Bunny.

BUNNY: Lyle, can you tell us how it feels to be the only member of the Harmony family who's not in the slammer?

HARRY: If I might, let me rephrase the question. What we're wondering, Lyle, is, well,

171

some people are saying that maybe you should be in the clink with your brothers and sisters, being as you've kept quiet about their secrets all these years. How do you respond to that?

IVAN: That's nonsense! Lyle doesn't belong in jail!

LYLE: It's okay, Ivan. It's a fair question. And it's something that's troubled me for years. I knew the secrets about Dorothy's lip-synching and Dwayne's double identity. I knew my brothers and sisters weren't best friends. I've spent my whole life listening to them fight! But I thought if I could move them back here to the country, they wouldn't do anybody any harm. Obviously I was wrong. They poisoned my dog. They tried to kill me. And worst of all, they treated these kids like dirt. If I'd have known how bad it was, I'd have done something about it.

CHARLOTTE: But what could you have done, Lyle? If you had told us their secrets, you would've had to turn the camp over to Dorothy. And then she would've just sold it and taken the Harmony show back on the road and conned all those thousands of fans.

CHARLIE: Like our parents.

BUNNY: Like me.

LYLE: I'm just thankful these kids figured out the secrets on their own.

JEWELY GEMS: Well, I'm relieved they're alive, the poor dears.

CHUCK ROAST: But look how skinny they've gotten! I say we all go get us some barbecue -- my treat!

HARRY: One last question, please. Kids, do you plan to keep in touch once you return home?

BARBIE Q.: Of course! Aren't we, y'all?

CAMPERS (ALL): YES!

BRISKET: And Lyle, you'll write, too, won't you?

LYLE: I will. And that's a promise.

July 30

Persons

weekly

HELLO, FAME!

Inside: Do the Lyle! See page 161 for a step-by-step guide to the dance craze that's sweeping the nation!

GOODBYE, FRIENDS!

The Stroganoff Scandal:
An Exclusive Report
Interviews with parents:
"Had we but known..."

Paige Turner
Publisher

August 15

Mr. Ivan Gems
Ms. Mimi Gems
34, Old Manse Road
London, England

Dear Ivan and Mimi,

I enjoyed meeting you last week in London. The stories you tell of Camp Happy Harmony are staggering, to say the least. Let me repeat how very interested we are in turning your adventures at Camp Happy Harmony into a best-selling book.

Ivan, as we discussed, this will entail a considerable amount of work on your part. I would like you to track down all the letters you and the other campers sent to your parents and to each other while at camp, as well as the Trans-Lake Mail sent by the Harmonys (those crooks!). The letters and notes must then be arranged in some sort of readable order. I have no idea how much time this will require, Ivan. But I know you're up to the task. After all, you and your friends cracked the case of the century!

And Mimi, I can think of no better cover for this book than a painting by you. Something similar to the wonderful mural you and your campmates painted in the Melody Mansion, perhaps? Or maybe an expressionistic painting of the young heroes of Camp Happy Harmony? Use your imagination.

I'd like to get this book on the shelves immediately, so please send the manuscript and artwork to me as soon as you're finished.

I look forward to seeing you on the best-seller list.

Nonfictionally yours,

Paige Turner
Publisher

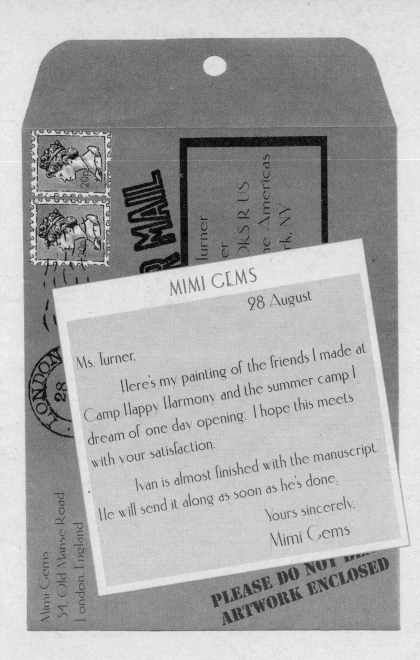

MIMI GEMS

28 August

Ms. Turner,

Here's my painting of the friends I made at Camp Happy Harmony and the summer camp I dream of one day opening. I hope this meets with your satisfaction.

Ivan is almost finished with the manuscript. He will send it along as soon as he's done.

Yours sincerely,

Mimi Gems

Mimi Gems
34 Old Manse Road
London, England

PLEASE DO NOT B...
ARTWORK ENCLOSED

WELCOME ABOARD
CAMP HEALTHY DISCORD!

BARBIE Q. ROAST
Stable master &
fashion designer

CHARLOTTE LEE
Dance instructor

MIMI GEMS
Artist-in-residence

BRISKET ROAST
Executive chef

CHARLIE LEE
Music maestro

IVAN GEMS
Writer-in-residence

Camp Healthy Discord is a place for brothers and sisters to spend a few weeks in the summer. We won't guarantee you'll like your brother or sister any better when you leave our camp. That's up to you. (And frankly, we don't trust kids who don't fight at least a little bit with their siblings.) What we do guarantee is that you'll have fun and meet kids from all over the world.

STAFF: Camp Healthy Discord is a kid-owned and operated camp. Our entire staff consists of kids. The only exception is Lyle Harmony, and he's really the biggest kid of all. Lyle delivers camp mail to both sides of Lake Lyle — by canoe.

FASHIONS: You can wear whatever you want at Camp Healthy Discord. But if you want a sneak peek at next year's hottest fashions, you've

come to the right place. Our camp is the summer workshop for designer Barbie Q. Roast, creator of Barbie Bibs. She'll make a pair of custom-fit overalls for you, or teach you how to design your own clothes. ❶

MOBILE PRISON: Remember those wicked Harmonys? Well, they're where they belong — in prison. And listen to this: The judge decided to lock them all away together in that la-

di-da tour bus Dorothy designed. Don't worry, though. They got their wish. The Harmonys now spend half the year on the road, traveling from city to city. They can't leave the bus, but people can come see the Harmonys and learn from their example how brothers and sisters should NOT behave. When it's not on tour, the mobile prison is parked on the grounds of Camp Healthy Discord. ❷

MUSIC MANSION: Here's where you'll find our recording studio and music maestro, Charlie Lee. Charlie will teach you how to compose and record songs. Or if you just want to listen to your own music, you can do that, too. We like all kinds of music — with obvious exceptions. **3**

DANCE HALL: Charlotte Lee creates and teaches the latest dance steps here in our dance hall. Our springboard floor is ideal for jumps and spins. You'll learn new dances and have a chance to make up your own moves. **4**

WRITING WORKSHOP: Novelist wannabes will want to spend time with Ivan Gems, our writer-in-residence. He'll help you get started writing your first book. Mysteries are his speciality. **5**

MEALS: World-class chef Brisket Roast prepares all meals served at Camp Healthy Discord. If you're interested in learning how to cook, talk to Brisket. He'll show you how to make grilled peanut butter pizza and apple pie pancakes. Breakfast and lunch are served indoors in Le Roastery. Evening meals are served al fresco, under the stars, at the Hideaway Café. **6**

MAIL: You can write to us at Camp Healthy Discord. Send all mail in care of Lyle Harmony. He'll take care of the rest. We have a rule at Camp Healthy Discord that campers must write at least one (1) Camp-O-Gram per week. If you need help, visit Ivan in the Writing Workshop. Besides teaching good manners, writing letters will help you next year in English class. And it might even land you a book deal!

LYLE HARMONY
Postmaster

CABINS: Boys' cabins are on the east side of Lake Lyle. Girls stay on the west side. **7**

TELEPHONES: Telephones are available at all times, though we prefer to communicate with Camp-O-Grams sent by Trans-Lake Mail. (It's just more fun to get a letter than a phone call.)

ACTIVITIES: You name it, we've got it. Swimming, dancing, singing, sewing, painting, reading, writing, cooking, eating and boating. If you can think of an activity we don't have, please let us know. We'll try to find a camper who can teach us and add the activity to our program.

NATURE TRAILS: Feel free to explore our 200-acre property. We love learning about the flora and fauna in the Ozarks, especially when we can study the wilderness while riding one of our burros! See our stable master Barbie Q. for details.

LAKE LYLE: Our crystal-clear lake is ideal for swimming, boating and fishing. Our friend Lyle Harmony will teach you how to bait a hook and cast a line. Lyle offers canoeing lessons daily. **8**

ART STUDIO: Looking for Mimi Gems? If she's not on a ladder somewhere painting a mural, she's probably in her studio. Mimi can teach anyone how to draw, paint and sculpt. **9**

34, Old Manse Road
London, England

Charlotte Lee
Rural Route 1, Box 257
Stopsign, IL

C. Roast
Chuck Roast Ranch
Porterhouse, Texas

Ms. Jewely Gems
34, Old Manse Road
London, England

Lyle Harmony
Camp Happy Harmony
301 Melody Lane
Harmony Hills, MO

C & C
RR 1, Box 257
Stopsign, IL

The Gems
34, Old Manse Road
London, England